DIRTY
TOGETHER

Book Three of the The Dirty Billionaire Trilogy

Meghan March

Editor: Pam Berehulke, Bulletproof Editing
www.bulletproofediting.com

Cover design: @ By Hang Le
www.byhangle.com

Photo: @ Sara Eirew
www.saraeirew.com

Formatting: Champagne Formats
www.champagneformats.com

ISBN: 978-1-943796-93-9

Visit my website at www.meghanmarch.com.

ABOUT THIS BOOK

My wife.

I love saying those words.

She's mine, and if she thinks I'm going to let her run without tracking her down and bringing her back to where she belongs—with me—then she's about to be introduced to a new reality.

Because I'll fight dirty to give her the happily-ever-after she deserves.

Dirty Together is the final book in The Dirty Billionaire Trilogy and should be read following *Dirty Billionaire* and *Dirty Pleasures*.

 ACKNOWLEDGMENTS

It takes a fabulous team to coax a spark of an idea along the twisty and crazy path to becoming a finished novel, and I'm lucky to have an amazing one.

Special thanks go out to:

Angela Smith of Grey Ghost Author Services, LLC, my amazing PA and best friend. It's been a wild ride, but this is only the beginning. I'm so proud of you and blessed to have you in my life.

Angela Marshall Smith and Pam Berehulke, editors extraordinaire, for once again helping me deliver the best story I'm capable of writing.

Chasity Jenkins-Patrick, kick-ass publicist, for talking me off more than one ledge and always pushing me in the right direction.

Natasha Gentile, for being a fabulous beta reader. Love your messages, lady!

Sara Eirew for shooting a fab cover pic, and By Hang Le for the absolutely gorgeous cover design.

The Meghan March Runaway Readers Facebook group, for being the most fabulous collection of ladies I've had the pleasure of (virtually) meeting. Hope to hug you all at events soon!

All the book bloggers who take the time to read and review this and any of my other books. Your time and dedication are truly appreciated.

My readers—I'm infinitely grateful that you've picked up this book. Without you, I wouldn't be living my dream.

CHAPTER ONE

Holly

I wait my turn at the single blinking red light in Gold Haven, Kentucky, and turn left before pulling into the gas station. This is the first place I ever pumped gas in my life. It was a lot cheaper then too. My Pontiac isn't a whole lot nicer than the 1988 Fiero I drove back then, but in this town, it doesn't stand out, and that's exactly what I need. I tug on a trucker hat and slip on sunglasses before opening the door and climbing out.

The old pumps I expected, the ones where the numbers click over as you fill up, have been replaced with newer models.

Even better. It lowers the chance that someone will recognize me if I can avoid all human interaction.

I swipe my card, get my gas, and twist the gas cap back

on. When I get back to Nashville, I'm finally going to look into replacing this car. I rarely splurge on anything.

Even though I won a "million-dollar recording contract" on *Country Dreams*, the amount I saw was laughable. Albums? They're expensive as hell to produce. And as far as the pay I get per show when I'm on tour, after all the expenses are covered? It's also nothing to write home about. But as my share of the ticket sales goes up and I build my fan base, that will eventually change.

But for now, I'm saving every penny I can and getting by on the bare minimum because I don't know when the bottom will fall out.

Not much has changed about that since I married billionaire Creighton Karas. Thoughts of my husband spiral through me, followed by equal jabs of guilt and regret. I can't believe I did it again. This morning I just up and walked out.

I don't know what I was thinking beyond . . . if I didn't get out of that penthouse at that very moment, I felt like something inside me was going to break. I had to get out of that city. I know I'm a coward and an idiot. No one has to tell me that because I've already called myself every name in the book.

I tear the receipt off and tuck it into my coat pocket before slipping back into my car. I turn the key.

Click.

I try it again.

Clunk.

Shit. I sigh, releasing a huge breath, and drop my forehead against the steering wheel.

This is karma, I'm pretty sure. This is what happens to women who leave their husbands—not once, but twice—without an actual explanation.

Crap. As much as I want to indulge in a pity party, now isn't really the time.

I gather myself, haul my purse over my shoulder, and push the car door open again. This place used to provide full-service fill-ups, but they discontinued those about the time I was learning to drive—not that I would have paid the extra two cents a gallon for the luxury.

I check my trucker hat to make certain it's secure before crossing the small lot and turning the corner to the side of the building where the garage bays are. Both overhead doors are closed, probably due to the howling wind, so I pull open the cloudy glass door and step inside the waiting room.

Creedence Clearwater Revival is jamming so loud you'd think you were standing right next to the stage at Woodstock. The cheap wood-paneled walls I remember from before have been replaced with metal diamond plating and spiffy blue paint that matches the outside of the building. The gas station has definitely gotten a makeover since the last time I was in town.

I ding the bell, but it can't be heard over the ringing guitar riffs.

I don't listen to enough CCR. But the fact that I could use a couple more upbeat songs takes second place to the fact that I need to have a vehicle that works, and there are no employees in sight here. I decide to take matters into my own hands and sneak behind the counter to the doorway that leads to the garage.

Inside, the smell of oil, exhaust, and rubber fills the air. Not unpleasant, but very *real*. It's darker in here, so I pull my sunglasses off and balance them on the bill of my hat.

My attention snags on the man bent over, turning a wrench under the hood of a classic Mustang. He's wearing coveralls tied around his waist, and a black thermal shirt stretches across his broad shoulders.

"Hey. Can I ask you a question?" My voice loses the battle against the volume of the music. "Hey!" I yell. Still no response.

I scan the room, locate the stereo, and march over to it. I slap my hand on the power button, and the music cuts off mid-lyric.

The man jerks up and turns to look toward the now silent stereo. "What the hell?" he barks, his eyes catching on me and staring intently. "Who the hell do you—"

"Sorry. You couldn't hear me over the music." I turn to face him fully, taking a few steps closer. I open my mouth to apologize again, but recognition sets in. "Logan Brantley?"

His narrowed eyes widen. "Holly Wickman. Haven't seen you in a coon's age." He pulls a rag from the back pocket of the coveralls and wipes his hands. He looks like he's about to hold one out for me to shake, but looks down at it and frowns.

"Hold on a sec." He turns on his heel and strides to the sink in the corner.

The scent of citrus cuts through the oil and exhaust,

and I realize he's scrubbing his hands clean before he offers me one. I'm not sure whether I'm embarrassed or flattered. After all, Logan Brantley was the premier bad boy of all bad boys, and I've crushed on him since I was old enough to crush on boys.

He never looked my way, though.

Older than me by a few years, he cruised around in his vintage Camaro like a badass, always with a different girl in the front seat. I was beneath his notice, and then he lit out of town as soon as they handed him a diploma. I had no idea he was back, and I can't help but wonder how the years have treated him.

He finishes washing and comes back to me, the scent of orange clinging to him.

"Of all the gin joints . . . What the hell are you doing in my garage, Holly Wix?" He throws my stage name in this time, and the heat of embarrassment creeps up my neck.

I lick my lips, rough from the heat of my car blasting on them during the blur of a drive from Nashville. I turned my radio up nearly as loud as it would go and started belting out the lyrics to every country oldie I could find. Anything to distract me from thoughts of Creighton, and how he might have reacted when he found the note. The voice in my head that sounds like Mama says he's just going to write me off this time.

"Holly?" Logan drags me back to the present.

"Sorry. I, um, my car won't start. I was getting gas, and then I got back in and turned the key, and just nothing. Well, a *click*, but then nothing." I snap my mouth shut when he grins, because I think he's laughing at the fact

5

that I'm babbling like an idiot.

"A *click*. Bad starter then, probably." He cranes his head toward the overhead doors. Trying to see my car, maybe? "What kind of hot ride you got these days? I could see you in a Lexus. You always were classier than the other girls around here."

My eyebrows shoot up. "Me? Classy?"

I wore hand-me-downs from the ladies at church who had daughters a few years older than me until I was sixteen and moved up to shopping at the ultra-discount stores. Maybe he's referring to the fact that I kept my boobs and butt covered, unlike some of the girls who scored that ride in his Firebird.

What's he going to think when he gets a look at my Pontiac? I'm going to blow his Lexus theory right out of the water. I'm still the same Holly I was before; the fringe and glitter of Nashville haven't changed me yet. Nor have the couple of weeks of being tied to Creighton's billions.

Logan's eyes fix on mine again. "Yeah, you. You've always been a class act. Although these days, I'm probably wrong about the Lexus. I bet you're rollin' in a Bentley." His reference to Creighton's money is impossible to miss, as is the slow, measuring look he gives me. "Yeah, I could see a Bentley suiting you just fine."

I'm not sure why he's so impressed. I'm wearing washed-out skinny jeans, a heather-blue thigh-length sweatshirt, a short black leather jacket, cowboy boots, and my trucker hat. Not exactly runway couture here.

"No Bentley. No Lexus." Although Creighton has a chauffeur-driven Bentley, it's not mine. So I might as well burst Logan's bubble quickly.

He shrugs. "All-righty then. Let's go see what we're working with."

I follow him out, almost slamming into his back when he stops short in front of the Pontiac.

"Please, woman, tell me that ain't your ride."

I pull my shoulders back and brazen it out. "Sorry it's not up to your standards."

He jerks his head to the side to get a look at me. "It ain't up to *your* standards—that's the problem."

I shrug. "The high life isn't always as glamorous as you'd think."

He mutters something under his breath, and I don't catch all of it. What I do catch sounds like *sorry excuse for a husband.*

"Keys?" He holds out a hand, and I drop them into it.

He has to adjust the seat way back before he can squeeze into the car. When he slides the key in the ignition and turns it, there's nothing. Not even a click or a clunk.

"Um, there was a clunk too. After the click."

"Yep. Starter or the solenoid's shot. I can order one, but I won't be able to get the part until Monday at the earliest. Maybe Tuesday."

Considering it was going on five o'clock on Saturday, I wasn't surprised by this.

"Okay. I really appreciate it."

He climbs back out of the car. "Happy to help out the hometown girl who made good. I'll get Johnny from the gas station to help me push it into the garage."

"Thank you. Seriously. That's one less thing to worry about then." *Except for how the hell I'm going to get to Gran's*, I add mentally.

I'm exhausted from the long day, but I pop the trunk anyway and haul out my bag. I round the car to the passenger side door and collect my purse. Hooking the strap over my shoulder, I shut the door and start around the hood.

Logan throws a hand out in a "stop" gesture. "What the hell are you doing?"

My eyes cut to his. "Going to Gran's house."

"On foot?"

"It's not that far."

"It's cold as shit, and it's at least three miles if it's a step. You ain't walking."

I bristle at his pronouncement. *Lord above, save me from alpha males.*

"I'm not sure when you decided it was cool to make decisions for me, but I'm just going to do whatever the hell I want, thanks."

"Holly, don't be ridiculous."

My temper flares hot and fierce. All thoughts of previous embarrassment are shoved right out the window.

"Do you not recognize the signs of a woman about to break? Because I'm hanging on by a thread here, and the last goddamn thing I need is another man telling me what I can or can't do." My voice has climbed an octave and a half by the time I finish snapping the words out.

"Whoa. Honey. Calm—"

"Don't even . . ."

He holds up two hands in front of him, as if warding

off the she-beast taking shape before him. "I'll give you a ride. If you want." He hastily tacks on that last bit, and I can feel my anger draining away as I agree.

"Okay. Thank you."

Logan tugs my bag from my hand, and I don't fight him. I'm whipped. Dog tired. Worn out. I just want to get to Gran's so I can face-plant on what I hope to God are clean sheets, and hibernate for a few days.

We pull out of the service station in Logan's big black jacked-up Chevy truck. The seats are dark gray leather, and it smells new. I scan the interior, looking for a dangling pine tree air freshener labeled New-Car Smell, but I don't see one. The electronics are so fancy that I think it must be new. Apparently Logan Brantley is the one living large these days.

He flips on the radio—to a country station, of course— and heads out of "downtown" toward my gran's. I do the mental quote-y fingers around "downtown" because it's one blinking red light and four corners. Given that the people of Gold Haven, Kentucky, aren't all that creative, they just refer to downtown as the Four Corners. There's the beauty shop corner, the pharmacy/post office corner, the pub corner, and the service station corner. That's the sum total of the Four Corners.

The radio DJ's voice catches my attention when he says my name. My latest single comes on. I should be giddy over the fact that I'm getting airplay, but all I can manage right now is a slight smile. I didn't come home to be Holly Wix.

Logan looks at me as if he's expecting me to say something, so I mumble the first thing that comes to me. "Guess you know you've made it when you hear yourself on your hometown radio station."

Logan shakes his head. "That's satellite. Local station plays you all the damn time. Don't play much else."

"Oh." The word comes out shaky.

He's looking out the windshield when he says, "I always knew you'd make something of yourself. Glad you took your shot when you had the chance." He glances sidelong at me before adding, "Even if it did put you out of my reach."

I'm so blown away by the surreal situation I find myself in—back in Gold Haven, riding in Logan Brantley's truck—that I can't even fumble for a response.

Apparently Logan doesn't mind, because he continues. "So, what the hell are you doing here, looking like you been rode hard and put up wet?"

I choke out a laugh and raise an eyebrow. "And here I thought you said I looked good."

He smiles, glancing toward me again and then back at the road. "Oh, you do, but you look tired, strung out—and you're short a husband."

I ball up my left hand and cover the rock with my right palm. Here in Kentucky, it seems even more obscenely large.

"I just needed a break," I say. "I needed to step away for a little while and sort some stuff out. By myself."

Logan flips on the blinker and turns right into Gran's gravel drive before slowing the truck to a stop close to the house and shifting into Park. He turns toward me in his seat.

"I would've thought this was the last place you'd come running to."

A million memories await me inside this house—and whatever mess Mama left behind after she broke in and helped herself to some of Gran's most prized possessions.

I take a breath, my shoulders rising, and then let it out slowly, straightening. "I guess when you decide to make a run for it, the most natural place in the world to run is back to your roots. I've only been gone nine months, but so much has changed. I wanted a bigger life, and boy, did I ever get it."

I don't even think before I speak, the truth of my feelings spilling out of me.

"But it's gotten so big, it's like I don't know who I am anymore. I thought if I came back here, maybe that would give me the answers I can't seem to find anywhere else."

"You made a run for it?"

I'm not surprised that's the part he picks up on. "It's a long story."

Hoping to leave it at that, I reach for the handle and push the door open before jumping down to the ground. *Practically need a damn stepladder for that thing.*

I hoist my purse up one more time and meet Logan at the front of the truck where he's holding my bag. He follows me up the front steps to Gran's purple porch.

She picked that color the summer before she passed because she was banking on it pissing off her crotchety old neighbor. She was right. Gran was *always* right. I guess the real reason I came back is because I'm hoping I can find her guidance and wisdom here, even if she's not.

I unlock the dead bolt and push the front door open. Dust motes float in the air. I guess getting picked up and tossed in jail got in the way of Mama doing some cleaning.

Logan drops my bag just inside the front door. He takes a step back, and I slip inside.

"Thanks. For the ride and for the help with the car. You can leave a message on Gran's machine when it's ready. I'll be checking it."

"Ain't no trouble." He's standing with his thumbs hooked into the waistband of his coveralls, and I have no idea what he's waiting for.

I start to push the door closed, but Logan says, "Be ready at eight."

"Wha—what?"

"You heard me."

"But I . . . What?"

"You came back to find your roots, Holly. I'm gonna reintroduce ya."

CHAPTER TWO

Holly

I told myself I wasn't going to go as I crawled under the clean sheets of my old bed and didn't set an alarm. I told myself I wasn't going to go while I ignored the high-pitched chime of the doorbell at seven forty-five. I told myself I wasn't going to go while I covered my head with a pillow to muffle the pounding coming from the door.

I told myself I wasn't going to . . . until Logan Brantley was standing in the doorway of my old bedroom.

Stunned, I shot up in bed. "What the hell? How'd you get in here?"

"Told you I was coming at eight. Figured you wouldn't be ready, so I came early. Now get your ass out of bed. We got places to go tonight."

"What part of me ignoring you for the last fifteen

13

minutes hasn't clued you in to the fact that I'm not going?"

He strolls into my room as if he's right at home and leans against the lilac-printed wallpaper. "You came here for a reason. I recognize someone looking to hide away and lick her wounds, but that don't help much. Trust me. I know."

I push the covers down, thankful I opted to sleep in my sweatshirt and some leggings. "You're really going to drag me out of here?"

"Kicking and screaming, if I have to. Given that any picture of you is going to end up online somewhere, you might want to fix your makeup."

My jaw drops, and I blink at his blatant honesty. "Jesus, it'd be a wonder if you had a girlfriend. You've got zero tact."

His lips quirk into a lopsided smile. "Maybe I've got more than one. Tact isn't exactly what the ladies are looking for these days, Wix."

"Whatever. Get out of my room." I jerk my head toward the door, in case he isn't getting the message loud and clear.

Logan laughs, and I can't help but appreciate that the man grew up real nice. He changed out of his shop clothes into worn jeans and a clean thermal Henley, this time in a deep forest green. From the way it stretches across his chest, I can tell the man is built.

I might be a married woman, but I'd be doing the sisterhood a disservice if I didn't take a minute to appreciate the fine specimen in front of me from an academic standpoint. I make a shooing gesture with my hands, and he finally turns and walks out . . . and I'm obligated to appreciate the back view as well.

Shaking my head, I swing my legs over the edge of the bed and reach into my bag. I pull out a pair of jeans and a longish black sweater. I search until it becomes clear that I didn't pack any socks. *At least I remembered to bring underwear.* That reminds me of being backstage with Creighton and him freaking out when he thought I didn't have any, and that I'd have to do my show in a dress without panties.

Why is it we seemed to find our rhythm in the midst of the craziness that's touring, but as soon as we step foot back in his world, I nearly have a nervous breakdown? What does that say for our future?

I push away the insistent question. I've got time to figure this out. I just need to get right with myself before I can start trying to figure out the rest. So instead, I head for the bedroom bureau and score some socks alongside the other odds and ends I left and never came back for.

I've been meaning to come back and clean the house out and sell it, but something always stops me—and not just the general lack of time in my schedule. When I wrote a check for the property taxes a couple of months ago, I told myself it was time.

But I haven't been able to pull the trigger. Even now, I'm not quite ready to let go. Which is ironic because in so many ways, I couldn't wait to shake the dust from this town off my boots. And once Gran was gone . . . coming back was too overwhelming. And yet, like I said to Logan, it was the only place I thought to run. Life is funny that way.

I, being the Kentucky girl that I am, recall a line from the movie *Days of Thunder*. Tom Cruise's nemesis, Rowdy Burns—the guy who becomes his friend after they smash their rental cars all up on the way to dinner—says something about how as a kid he farmed so he could race, but later he was just racing so he could get back and live on the farm. At least I think it went something like that.

It may not be some classy, iconic movie quote, but it always stuck with me. Just one more way of saying the grass is always greener on the other side. I'm not in the same position as Rowdy Burns, because I don't have some burning desire to come back to Gold Haven permanently, but I can't help but wonder if, someday in the future, I'll be singing and touring my ass off to save enough to quit.

It's unfathomable.

I freeze in the act of pulling a sock on. *Did I just imagine my future without Creighton in it?* Because if Creighton is part of my future, money surely isn't an object, right?

And then comes the bigger questions: if Creighton is part of my future, will I still be touring and singing ten years from now? Even if this does work between us, at what point is he going to think the country music gig—while cute—is getting old?

Stop borrowing trouble, Holly. I make a conscious decision to bury the questions again for tonight. I'm not ready to answer them yet. Maybe having Logan show up at my doorstep was some kind of serendipity in the form of a welcome distraction.

Stripping out of my leggings, I pull on the jeans and

trade the sweatshirt for the sweater, and look at my reflection in a mirror that saw me through the awkwardness of my teen years. It's easy to catalog all the ways I look different now.

My hair is longer and shinier—courtesy of using the products my stylist recommended and not Suave. My entire body is slimmer—thanks to the restrictive diet and calorie counting. But would you believe that my boobs are perkier? No, I didn't sell my soul to the devil; I discovered the miracle of push-up bras and was actually fitted for one in my size. My face, to go along with my slimmer body, is narrower, my cheekbones sharper, and my eyebrows have been professionally shaped. But beyond that, I'm still the exact same girl I was when I left.

Is that girl ever going to be enough for Creighton?

"Stop it," I scold my reflection. "Just stop."

"Hurry up, Holly!" Logan yells up the stairs, interrupting me.

"Hold your horses, you breaking-and-entering fool," I yell back.

I grab my makeup bag and use the concealer to cover the circles under my eyes, and then add a swipe of bronzer over my cheeks and another coat of mascara and lip gloss. That'll have to be good enough.

Logan's idea of reintroducing me to my roots starts with food at Mr. Burger, the only fast-food joint in town since McDonald's won't bother setting up a franchise here. It's surprisingly quiet for a Saturday night, but that suits me just fine.

We order and slip into a back booth to wait for the server to bring out our food. The joke around town is that Mr. Burger's is so slow because they have to go kill the cow first.

It's twenty minutes before two loaded cheeseburgers, seasoned fries, and chocolate milkshakes are sitting in front of us. I haven't consumed this many calories in one sitting . . . probably since the last time I ate here. This meal is miles away from the decadent steak that Creighton ordered in our hotel room.

The food is *amazing*. The company isn't half bad either.

I don't have much to say, but Logan fills the silence, even though I get the feeling he's not normally this chatty of a guy. He tells me about coming back to town after leaving the Marines. He won't say exactly what it is he *did* in the Marines, so I suspect it was something interesting.

He came back to town just days after I left for Nashville, and knew he couldn't be idle, so he applied for a job at the garage he worked at all through high school. Apparently he spent a lot of his down time in the service restoring classic cars, so Chuck, the prior owner, hired him back on the spot.

"When Chuck told me he planned to retire about three months later, I knew that I couldn't let him sell it to someone else. Coming back to that damn garage was the best homecoming I had. He wasn't surprised at all that I didn't want him to sell it to anyone else, and was cool enough to help me buy it from him. I've almost got him paid off, so the bank loan for the renovations was a leap of faith. It's turning out just fine, though."

I'm amazed that in six months he's managed to buy the place, renovate the whole thing, and turn Chuck's old garage into a sought-after place for classic car restoration and repairs. To say I'm impressed would be an understatement. It appears that I'm not the only one who's capable of going after a dream.

I'm also slightly stunned that we get out of Mr. Burger without being bothered. I guess I'm not such a big deal, even in my own town. Apparently only Miranda Lambert is famous in a small town.

Act II of Operation Reintroduce-Holly-to-Her-Roots takes us right back to the place it all started—Brews and Balls. I should have figured, since it's really the only place for people to go for entertainment in Gold Haven.

The reception I get there is much different than at Mr. Burger. You'd think I'm the returning hero who has been away for years and years, which clearly, I'm not.

"Hot damn, look what the cat dragged in," Benny yells over the percussion of balls hitting the lane and striking pins. He shuffles over as fast as his cane can hold him, and yanks me into a hug.

"Hey, Ben. How ya been?" It's the same way my gran greeted him for years, and it rubbed off on me long ago.

He pulls back, lowers the old wooden cane back to the floor to steady himself, and tilts his head to one side. "I think I'm more interested in how *you've* been, Mrs. Billionaire Country Star."

Heat burns in my cheeks. I don't want to talk about the me that exists outside this town. That's not why I'm here.

"I'm fine. Just taking some time off."

He opens his mouth to ask something else, but shuts it just as quick. I glance sideways at Logan, and he's giving Benny a hard look. Shielding me from questions?

"How about some shoes and a lane, Ben?" Logan asks.

The older man nods enthusiastically. "Of course. Anything for my girl here. Except, there's a catch."

"Ben—" Logan starts, but I interrupt. I know exactly what Benny's going to throw out as the catch.

"I'll sing one song. But not one of mine."

"Done. Go bowl a few games, and I'll meet you in the bar later."

We bowl two games, and the easy camaraderie I feel with Logan surprises me. It's not the heightened anticipation I seem to have every moment I spend around Creighton, but it's also a lot less stressful.

It's just . . . easy.

It's also impossible not to compare the men, one rough around the edges and the other smooth and cultured. Both dangerous in their own way.

I know how to behave around a guy like Logan, and not just because I've spent a lot of time with Boone on tour. Logan's upbringing wasn't all that different from mine. I can throw sass at him and give as good as I get, all without feeling awkward or trashy.

I give as good as I get with Creighton too, but when I'm in his world, I lack confidence because I'm totally out of my element. On tour, things were better, but that was him playing in my world. Wasn't there some old saying about a bird and a fish falling in love? Are we just too different?

My thoughts are distracting enough to make me throw a gutter ball. *Damn.* There goes my three-hundred game, which I'm perfectly capable of bowling, thank you very much. And that's just another skill a billionaire's wife probably shouldn't have on her résumé.

I excel at bowling, deep-frying pickles, and singing songs about pickup trucks and broken hearts. I hate feeling like this, so inadequate, and I hate that I'm the one digging the slices in deeper. How can I ever truly be good enough for Creighton if I never believe it myself? Annika's words jab at me again and again.

Logan throws a strike, thankfully distracting me yet again. He can also bowl a three hundred. I watched him on plenty of dates when I worked here in school. Just another difference between the two men. Brews and Balls is the kind of place a guy like Logan brings a date. I try to picture Creighton here and find it utterly impossible.

But I was so determined to shake this place off and never come back, so what does it matter if I can't picture Creighton here? I wanted a bigger life, and I got it. When am I going to get the guts to *live* it instead of just float along and let the tide pull me in and out?

I grab my ball, line up . . . and throw another one into the gutter. Turning away from the lane, I drop into the molded blue plastic chair and rest my head into my hands.

"Holly, what the hell?" Logan asks.

"I can't do this. I need to stop thinking. I don't want to think any more tonight, and this isn't working."

Logan sets his ball back into the ball return and lowers himself into the seat beside me. Underlying the woodsy scent of his aftershave or deodorant is that combination from the garage—oil, exhaust, rubber, and citrus.

It's not unpleasant. It's *real*.

But it's not Creighton.

"What can I do? How do we get you to stop thinking?" he asks.

I can only think of one solution. "Let's get drunk."

Logan shakes his head. "I'm driving."

"Then *I'll* get drunk."

He doesn't speak for the space of a breath. Finally, he leans his elbows on his knees and looks sidelong at me. "You sure?"

"Abso-fucking-lutely." I may not know the answer to any other question I need to answer, but this one, I have handled. Like a boss.

With a shake of his head, he says, "Pick your poison then. And maybe get that song in for Ben before you're too lit to be able to sing it."

"I think tonight is a tequila kind of night. And I can *never* be too lit to sing." I scrunch my brow. "I don't think. I guess we'll see."

"Fuck, I know this is a bad idea." But go along with it, he does.

Shots are lined up on the bar, and I forgo the salt and the lime, opting instead to take my shots straight and chase them with beer. This decision is probably one I'll regret later. Almost certainly. But I'm already feeling the buzz and forgetting to care.

Benny is already cuing up a song when I grab the microphone from the stand. I don't even care what it is. I just want to get onstage, even if it's a tiny stage in a Podunk bowling alley, because this is one place I feel completely confident. I'm going to sing my heart out tonight. These people may have come to bowl and drink, but they're about to get one hell of a show.

The music that comes from the speakers makes me laugh, a real, honest-to-God belly laugh. Something I haven't done in longer than I can remember. Somehow Benny always knows where my head's at. He's cranked up Miranda Lambert's "Famous in a Small Town."

I belt out the lyrics and find my happy place.

Benny plays song after song, and the tequila keeps flowing. I don't count the songs or the shots, or the number of people gathering in the small bar of the bowling alley. I don't keep track of any of it. I don't notice the whispers of the crowd, the flashing cameras, or later, the people stepping aside to let someone pass.

My eyes are closed and tears are welling in them as I sing the last lines to Sara Evans's "Born to Fly." It's the song that started it all on this very stage. A little overwhelmed, I slide the microphone back into the stand and lean over, hands on my thighs, trying to reel myself back in.

"Another shot, Holly?" someone calls.

I hold my arm out, making a thumbs-up sign. And that's when I hear a familiar deep voice say, "I think you've had enough, my dear."

CHAPTER THREE

Creighton

You know what plays havoc with a man's ego? Having a wife who has walked out on him twice. Luckily, my ego is big enough to handle it. But these detective missions to find out where my wife has run off to are getting a little old.

Listening to her sing, however, will never get old. I stand at the back of the crowd in the karaoke bar of the bowling alley and get my first look at Holly on the stage where she found the courage to chase her dream.

She's fucking magnificent, and I'm far from the only person in the crowd to think so. These people, who she probably claims as *her* people, are in awe of her talent. Which they should be.

When the last note fades away, I move through the

crowd, making my way to the stage. I have no idea what I'm going to say, but I don't think it really matters. My being here should send a message all of its own.

"Another shot, Holly?" someone yells over the now cheering crowd, but Holly is bent over at the waist, trying to catch her breath—something I've never seen her do onstage. It appears my wife has had plenty of shots tonight.

Conscious of all the cameras flashing, I make an executive decision and step up to the stage. "I think you've had enough, my dear."

Her head jerks up and she meets my eyes. "That's not your call," she says, her words slurring.

"It is tonight. We're leaving."

"I'm not going back to New York. Not now."

I stiffen at her adamant statement. "I think we should save that discussion for when you're sober."

"Fine. But I'm not done."

She grabs the microphone from the stand and calls out, "How about one more?"

The crowd roars.

"Let's take it back to some classic Reba!" Holly yells. "I've got a craving for a little something 'Fancy.'"

The crowd roars again, this time to a deafening volume. The music starts to play, and I'm pretty sure I've heard the song, but I've never really listened to the lyrics before. But when Holly sings them, they sink into me one line at a time.

Everything she's said about her mother and running off with men who have enough money to take care of her for a little while comes filtering back into my brain. This song is a message to me, and I think I'm hearing it loud and clear.

What I don't know is how the hell I'm going to get through to her that she isn't just some kind of ornament in my life. She *is* my life.

Holly isn't a woman who will be swayed by words. I know that now. She needs me to show her. And guess what? That I can fucking do.

Her clear, stunning voice carries the last note for what seems like forever, and the bar thunders with applause and cheering. This time I don't wait. I step closer, swing her up into my arms, and jump down off the stage.

"What are you—?"

"I'm taking you home."

"I'm not going—"

"To *your* home, Holly."

"Oh."

Her arms twine around my neck, and she holds on tight while I maneuver us through the crowd and out of the bar, into the lobby of the bowling alley.

I feel a tap on my shoulder and glance back.

It's a guy. A big guy.

"She's done for tonight," I tell him. "You can get her autograph another time, man."

"If I wanted her autograph, I would've gotten it when I picked her up tonight."

Everything in me stills.

"Logan, it's okay—" Holly starts.

I don't even wait for her to finish her sentence. I turn and walk for the doors.

As soon as she said his name, a seething possessiveness shredded my better judgment. I have to get out of here before I put her down and take this guy on in a way that he'll understand—with my fists, until one or both of us are bleeding. I'm hoping, if he has any sense, he'll stay inside.

But I hear the heavy booted footsteps behind me as I carry Holly outside to my rental.

"You ain't just coming in here and carrying her out without me hearing from Holly's lips that she wants to go with you."

I left the car unlocked, figuring that no one was going to steal it. I grab the door handle and rip it open before depositing Holly inside and slamming it shut.

She yells something, but I slide my hand into my pocket and hit the Lock button before she can open it. In her drunken state, it'll take her a few moments to figure out how to unlock the fucking thing. *Thank you, Cadillac.*

I turn and face *Logan.* "Apparently I'm at a disadvantage, because you know who I am, but I'm pretty sure Holly has never mentioned anyone named Logan."

He crosses his bulky arms over his chest. He might have thirty pounds on me, but I'm used to sparring with Cannon. And there's the added factor of me being riled the fuck up and defending my claim to *my* woman. I'm not afraid to bleed to make a point.

"I ain't tryin' to get between a husband and wife—" he starts.

"Then turn around and head back inside."

He continues as if I didn't speak. "But I also don't be-

27

lieve in letting a woman I brought somewhere leave with another man."

I flex my hands and curl them into fists. "Well, you sure as fuck aren't leaving with her tonight. So you're going to have to put that belief on ice." Even in the dimly lit parking lot, I can see the muscle ticking in his jaw. "If you're looking to stake a claim on a woman, I suggest you pick one who's available."

He smirks. "The only reason you had a shot at her is because I *didn't* stake a claim."

"Then you missed your shot. The next time we're in town, I'll buy you a beer to thank you. Right now, I'd like to get my *wife* home before she pukes in my rental car." I say the word *wife* with undeniable emphasis and satisfaction.

"Seems to me a man with a wife like that should learn how to keep a hold on her a little better."

The words aren't that far off from what Boone said when he ripped me a new asshole several hours ago in Nashville.

"You better not keep doing shit that sends her running, or you're gonna fuckin' lose her for good," was Boone's redneck wisdom.

He made his point when he eyed the shotgun hanging above the front door, and when he delivered his final warning. *"That girl is one of the good ones. Don't make her cry, or I'll be forced to step in and take action. I consider her family."*

My explanations placated him enough for him to tell me exactly where she went. Back to the small town she came from is about the last place I would have thought to look, so I owe Thrasher. But I don't owe this asshole anything.

Logan narrows his eyes on me. "This conversation ain't done." He jerks his head toward the car door. "But it can wait."

I look at the car as well, and see Holly passed out against the window. *Shit.*

"You know how to get to her gran's place?" he asks, clearly deducing the problem I'm facing as soon as I do.

It's with annoyance I admit that I don't have a clue. He's in the middle of giving me directions when Holly rouses and knocks on the window.

Fuck. I recognize that look. I unlock the door and pull it open just in time for Holly to lean her head out and puke on the gravel. I step around the door and gather her hair into a messy ponytail behind her head. A car door opens and shuts nearby, but I'm not paying attention to anything but Holly.

Logan reappears, crouching just out of range of the vomit as he holds a bottle of water to her lips.

Given the caveman tendencies that spring to life every time I'm around Holly, I should be pissed to see another man helping take care of her, but I'm not. I'm grateful because taking care of her is the only thing that matters right now, not the pissing contest I was engaging in. It's amazing how simple things become when priorities are highlighted so brilliantly.

When she's finished drinking and puking and drinking again, I smooth Holly's hair away from her face and tuck it behind her shoulder. She sits back in the seat of the Cadillac and looks from me to Logan.

"I'm confused. And drunk." Her gaze swings back to me. "How the hell are you here? Why?"

"I think that conversation is best saved for when you'll actually remember what I say."

"Good. I don't know what to say yet . . ." Her words trail off as her eyes slide shut.

Fuck.

I snap my attention to Logan. "What the fuck did you do to her? I've never seen her like this."

"She was trying to forget about you."

His words are like a jab to my gut. I exhale sharply, physically feeling the effects of the verbal sucker punch.

"Well, that isn't fucking happening because I'm not going anywhere."

"Your choice, man, but if a woman asks me for space, I tend to give it to her if the alternative is pushing her away by refusing to give her what she needs."

"What is it with rednecks and their fucking need to dispense backwoods wisdom today?"

"I'd resent that if you hadn't just acknowledged that they're wise words."

I didn't mean to imply that, but this Logan guy is apparently smarter than he looks.

Holly slumps sideways, on the verge of falling out of the seat, and we both reach out a hand to steady her. He snatches his back when I shoot him a sharp look. Carefully, I sit Holly upright in the seat and close the door. Once she's situated, I turn to him.

That thought about my inner caveman calming down? Total bullshit. I need to make something clear to him before I drive out of here. And considering Holly needs to be in bed five minutes ago, I'll make it clear without wasting any time.

"You see that ring on her finger? That means she's not fair game, unless that's the kind of guy you are."

Logan's head jerks back, and his eyes narrow. "I ain't lookin' to poach. I respect that you took vows, but I also know that you don't have a good track record of keeping 'em."

Rage boils through me, and I fight the urge to plant my fist in his face. Age-old instinct has me stepping toward him until an old man comes shuffling through the parking lot and inserts his cane between us.

"All right now, boys. Time to get 'em out and measure, or get on home."

"I think I'll take the latter," I say.

I'm pretty sure I hear Logan mumble something about me losing in a dick-measuring contest, but the old man is already speaking again and holding up a purse I recognize as Holly's.

"You know where her gran's house is?" the old man asks me.

"Mostly." Logan's instructions were cut off midway through.

The old man nods. "You just need to take a right, go a half mile, and it's the first house on the left after the power lines. If you hit the railroad tracks, you've gone too far."

His decidedly country directions are easy enough. He

holds the purse up higher. "This is hers."

"Thank you," I say, reaching out to grab it, but the old man jerks it back before I can.

"You take care of that girl, or I'll have your balls in a sling."

Jesus fucking Christ. I don't even know what that means, but it's the third threat I've received today.

Snatching the purse out of his hand, I nod. "Duly noted." I turn for the car, but Logan isn't quite done yet.

"Her bedroom is the one at the top of the stairs. You can't miss it." His words are tinged with triumph, and once again I want to put him on his ass in this gravel parking lot.

"I don't want to know why you fucking know that." My voice comes out rough and deep, and I almost don't recognize it.

Logan smirks and tucks one thumb into the pocket of his jeans. "Calm down, rich boy. It ain't like I popped her cherry."

Why he's choosing to bait me now, I don't know, and I don't fucking care. I also don't want to drag my lawyer out to Bumfuck, Egypt, to bail me out of jail, even if the charges are justifiable homicide. So I take the high road; I threaten him.

"You do know I can afford to make you disappear, right?" I round the car and reach for the driver's side handle, pausing in anticipation of his response.

Logan leans against a black truck parked next to the Cadillac, and I'd bet my jet it's his. "Out here, a man does his own killin' and buryin'. I know miles of mine shaft where you'd never be found," he drawls.

I straighten and take his measure. "I get that you're a cocky son of a bitch, but what's your angle here?"

He meets my gaze without hesitation. "I didn't like the way Holly looked when she rolled into town, and you're the most likely cause."

I imagine her looking tired and stressed to the max, the way she did before everything went to shit last night at the MoMA event, and I want to get her back to her grandmother's house to take care of her properly. Last night left a lot to be desired on both our parts, but I'm here to fix whatever broke between us.

I keep my words steady, even as my temper flares hotter. "I don't see how that's any of your business."

Logan shifts his shoulders back, and his hands tighten into fists at his sides. "I'm making it my business."

I glance at Holly, passed out in the passenger seat, before looking back to Logan. "I don't have time for this right now, but if you've still got a death wish in the morning, you know where I'll be."

He shoves off the truck and steps toward me, and this time it's my hands balling into fists. "Some of us have to work in the morning. Like me, on your wife's piece-of-shit car that broke down the second she pulled into town."

I curse under my breath. "Don't bother fixing it. I'll buy her something when we get home." I don't know what she was driving, but I'm guessing it wasn't the Maserati I'd pick for her.

"You sure she's leaving with you?" Logan says smugly.

"Abso-fucking-lutely." I won't allow for any alterative

outcome.

"That's the same answer your wife gave when I asked her if she wanted to get drunk tonight."

I grit my teeth as I yank the door open. Logan is still leaning against his truck as I pull out of the parking lot of the bowling alley, gravel flying. I swear his smug smile grows bigger, and I hope the stones chipped the paint of his truck. Fucker.

We make it to Holly's gran's front porch before she starts puking again, and I know it's going to be a long night.

And tomorrow? Tomorrow, Holly and I need to have our own come-to-Jesus talk.

CHAPTER
FOUR

Holly

My head pounds and the light cutting across the room hurts my eyes, even though they're still closed. I make a sound that I think qualifies as a moan, but it's guttural enough to be an animal noise. Rolling my head to the side, I see a glass on the nightstand, and pills beside it.

"Thank you, Logan," I mumble.

I almost fall out of bed when a deep voice answers, "It wasn't Logan."

I shoot up in bed and regret it instantly as nausea roils in my gut. "Creighton?"

He's seated in the tiny chair that belongs to my vanity. He looks ridiculous because he's big enough to crush it.

What the hell is he doing here?

My mind spins, looking for answers, and I can't grasp

a single one. My confusion must be obvious, because Creighton raises an eyebrow.

"You don't remember last night?"

Last night? My memory might as well be a black hole. I shake my head, and splinters of pain shoot from behind my eyeballs.

Whoa, Holly. Take it easy.

I look at Creighton once more, but his dark expression sends a new and different kind of pain through my head. It's a look I've seen before. *Creighton is pissed.* The reason for it comes out quickly.

"The fact that you expected another man to be in your bedroom pisses me the fuck off, Holly."

Big swamping waves invade my stomach, notching up the nausea at the thought of the coming confrontation— one I'm not nearly ready for—and I swing my legs off the bed and bolt into my tiny bathroom. Dry heaves rack my body until tears stream down my face.

A glass of water appears beside me magically. Well, if you consider Creighton Karas to be magic. I refuse to give my opinion on the matter.

Mumbling my thanks, I take a sip and spit it into the toilet. I feel like road kill, and not a single memory of last night surfaces from the black hole. *Not a good sign.*

Creighton takes the water from me and produces a damp washcloth before leaving the tiny bathroom.

I wipe my face and carefully stand. A peek in the mirror reveals that I also look like road kill resurrected from the dead.

I wipe at the raccoon eyes left by my mascara, and attempt to look less awful. My hair is tangled and knotted, so I grab a hair tie off the counter and attempt to pull it away from my face into some semblance of order, but it's really not happening. Nothing is going to touch this hot mess but a shower.

Wary, I poke my head out of the bathroom door. Creighton is sitting on my bed, looking completely out of place in my white and pale lilac room. His eyes are on me, and his pissed-off vibe hasn't lessened a bit.

"I, um, I'm going to grab a shower."

The nod he gives me is stiff, and I can't read anything beyond *not frigging pleased* in his expression.

Frowning, I slip back into the bathroom and shut the door. After stripping off my rumpled clothes, I turn the ancient showerhead all the way to Hot and hope it can wash away . . . something. Everything? I don't even know anymore.

I came here to get away, to regroup, but part of me is really happy to see Creighton in my bedroom. I thought I'd be ashamed to have him see this side of me, but something about it is actually . . . freeing?

Like I no longer have anything to hide. Like he's seen all of me, including the innermost and least fame-worthy part of me, and he's still here.

I smile into the nearly scalding water, and when I feel something like hope bubbling up inside me, I can't help but start singing in the shower.

After I brush the hell out of my teeth and my tongue is mostly numb from Listerine, I reach for the door handle. The smile on my face is wide, and I feel almost human again.

I'm ready to talk to Creighton, ready to lay out my cards and see if we can figure out where we go from here.

My room is silent and empty when I push open the door. I hang my towel on the back of my chair, and dig some yoga pants and a T-shirt out of my bag. Listening for sounds of life in the house, I pad down the stairs.

There's more silence when I enter the kitchen. My stomach churns, although it was calm only a few minutes ago, and I think I'm going to be sick again.

Creighton's gone, and there's no sign to suggest I didn't just imagine his presence.

With measured steps, I cross the room and peek out the lace curtains to the front yard and gravel drive.

Empty.

I don't remember what Creighton drove last night due to the memory thief called tequila, but I know he must have a car. There's no garage for it to hide in.

Which means . . . he's really gone.

Gone.

I stumble back from the window as the realization hits me.

Gone. I slide into a chair at the kitchen table that takes up the center of the room. My elbow smacks into the edge, and I wince at the pain shooting up my arm. My eyes sting with tears when I see the note that says simply:

DIRTY TOGETHER

Two words.

"What the hell?" I say to the empty room. "What does that mean?" I don't know why I ask the question, because the ivy-printed wallpaper isn't going to answer me.

Then it hits me. Two words. Each time I've left him, I left a note with two words: *Good-bye, Creighton.*

Is this just him being an asshole and making a point? I blink back the tears. I don't have time for tears.

It's then I see a guitar case leaning up against the wall in the corner, the same leather guitar case I left in the penthouse in New York. I push up from the table, my elbow still stinging, and take the few steps necessary to bring me to it. Crouching, I lay it flat on the floor, flick the latches, and lift the lid.

Inside is the Gibson, looking just as beautiful as it did the day it was delivered. But that's all that's inside the velvet case. There's no note or any other indication of what Creighton was thinking when he left it here.

I drop to my butt, lean my back against the stove, and lift the guitar into my lap. After strumming a few chords to make sure it's in tune, I begin to play.

The song I sing? It's the one I've poured all my insecurities into, the self-doubt that was temporarily beaten back when I was singing in the shower. "Lost on Fifth Avenue."

I slam my hand down on the strings midway through the second verse. *Screw. This.* I'm not going to sit in the corner and wallow in pity. I'm done throwing pity parties. Because what is that going to accomplish anyway? Not a thing. If I want to make something happen, I need to get off my butt and go do it.

I slide the guitar back into the case and shut it. Creighton and I need to hash things out, if it's not already too late. And damn it, if he left—*really* left—then it's my turn to track him down.

My purse is hanging off the back of the kitchen chair closest to me. I pull it down and dig around for my phone. It's not dead, which is a win. Finding Creighton's contact info, I hit Send. It rings twice and goes to voice mail.

Did he seriously hit Ignore? *On me? What the fuck?*

I call him again.

Rings once. Voice mail.

I text.

ME: Two words? Seriously? Two words?

I wait.

And wait.

And wait.

And *nothing*.

I'm being completely irrational; I know it. I have absolutely no right to be pissed about this. None. But knowing that doesn't stop me from feeling this way.

So I text him again.

ME: I've got two words for you, Crey. Care to guess what they are?

As soon as I hit SEND, I'm wishing I had an UNDO button. *Chill out, Holly.* But that doesn't mean I'm any less pissed.

A car door slams outside. Jumping up, I put down the phone and stalk to the door and yank it open. I freeze when it's not Creighton.

It's Logan, and he wastes no time nodding in greeting. "Good to see that you're alive and kickin' this morning. Was a little worried about you last night."

"Maybe you should've cut me off before I drowned myself in tequila and regret."

He smiles, not looking apologetic in the least. "You're a big girl. Figured you could make your own decision as to when you'd had enough."

"Thanks for the vote of confidence."

"You made it this far. Didn't think one drunk night back on your old stompin' grounds would derail you too much. Besides, the pictures of you online look pretty damn good."

"Pictures?" My voice comes out a little screechy. "Shit. I didn't even think . . ."

"Don't worry. The captions all say stuff about you having an impromptu concert in your hometown. Nothing scandalous."

My mind spins. "Since when do you google me and read all that stuff?"

If I expected him to be embarrassed by my question, I would be wrong.

His smile widens. "Since before you showed up at my shop in that piece-of-shit Pontiac."

Logan Brantley just admitted to stalking me online. I've entered the Twilight Zone.

"How long before?" I ask, my curiosity getting the better of me.

"On that one, I'm gonna have to plead the Fifth." He leans against the big black truck. "Was surprised to see the Caddy in the parking lot of Piggly Wiggly this morning."

Caddy? Piggly Wiggly? Those seem like two things that don't belong in the same sentence.

My confusion must be obvious because Logan adds, "You don't remember the Caddy? You damn near puked all over it. Barely got the door open in time. Karas's rental bill would've been a little bit higher then, not that he would've probably cared."

The picture is starting to come together, and sweet relief is flooding me. "Are you telling me that Creighton is at Piggly Wiggly?"

The mental image is comical. Creighton in a three-piece suit, pushing a shopping cart and picking up . . . what? Eggs and bacon?

Then what was with the note? Was that just a taste of my own medicine?

Logan shrugs. "That was my assumption, anyway."

I'm still trying to absorb this new development when the deep purr of an engine catches my attention, and a shiny black Cadillac crunches over the gravel drive, stopping next to Logan's truck.

The Caddy. Crey's rental car.

The man in question puts the car in PARK and opens the door. I can't read his expression when he steps out.

While we were on tour, I saw Creighton in jeans several times, but something about the denim clinging to his hips sucks IQ points straight out of my brain. The black thermal knit shirt hugging his broad shoulders and defined chest adds to the effect.

His diligence in keeping fit surprised me as well on tour. He and Boone bonded over weight lifting stuff that meant nothing to me. I was happy he developed an easy camaraderie with BT. It was another way he fit into my world that I didn't expect.

He glances at Logan. "Brantley. You need something?"

"Nothing at all. Just stopping in to see how Holly is feeling this morning."

Creighton nods and presses a button on the remote in his hand. The trunk lid pops open. "Might as well make yourself useful and carry in groceries before Holly tries to help."

Logan looks from me to Creighton and does exactly that. The men both carry in armfuls of grocery bags.

"Damn, you planning to feed the whole neighborhood?" Logan asks before pausing and adding, "Or are you planning on staying a while?"

"Staying as long as Holly wants." Creighton's response is matter-of-fact.

I'm following them up the steps of the front porch and trip as the words come out of his mouth. I would have fallen on my face, but Crey drops an armload of bags and grabs me before my forehead connects with the porch's

43

wood planks.

"Shit, Holly. Are you okay?" he asks as he carefully spins me to face him.

Stunned, I stare up into his dark brown eyes, wondering when everything changed. I expected him to still be furious, as furious as he looked this morning. But instead I'm caught up in the arms of a man who is looking at me like not letting me fall is the most important thing in his life.

No man has ever dropped anything—literally or figuratively—to catch me from falling.

So in that moment, my two options become very clear: continue to hold up my walls and be afraid to rest easy in the safety of his arms, or lean into him and let the walls crumble around me.

Blind trust is a new concept for me. Actually, it never occurred to me to trust a man. They rotated in and out of my childhood, and except for Ben, no man has ever shown me that my trust would be safely placed with him. But Creighton might as well be a breed of his own.

"Holly?" Crey asks again, and I realize I've totally checked out.

"Yeah. I'm fine. Sorry. Just . . . missed a step." *Maybe missed a lot more than a step.*

Creighton's stare intensifies. "I think we've both missed several steps. And that's something we're going to rectify."

He sets me on my feet and gathers up the bags. My gaze cuts to Logan, who is watching us both. His eyebrows are drawn together as if he's trying to dissect what the heck is going on.

I pull open the door, and the men both carry their bags inside. "You can just put them on the table."

Logan sets his down and looks to Creighton and then to me. "You need anything from me while you're in town, just holler. You still want me to fix up the car? It'll sell better if it runs."

"You can tow it to the junkyard. Holly will have a new car waiting for her in Nashville."

Okay, so maybe my trust is a gradual thing, and not so blind or immediate. Baby steps.

"Whoa. No one is selling my car or towing it to a junkyard. I need it."

Logan is leaning against the cupboard, and Creighton is standing near the wall. Both men are looking at me with nearly identical expressions.

"You can't drive that piece of shit," Logan says.

"Says who?" I ask.

"Says me," Creighton replies.

"Not your call." My tone is adamant.

Logan pushes off the cupboard. "This sounds like a domestic issue. I'll let you two sort it out." He touches the brim of his baseball cap. "Call me when you decide."

I open my mouth to tell him I've already decided, but Creighton moves to stand beside me and reaches down to thread his fingers through mine. When he squeezes lightly, the move silences me.

"Thanks, Brantley. We'll be in touch."

Logan crosses to the door, pulls it open, and gives us one last glance. He's smirking, and I'm pretty sure he's seeing something I'm not.

"See you around, Karas."

CHAPTER FIVE

Holly

When the door shuts behind Logan, I'm left in the kitchen with piles of Piggly Wiggly bags and my husband's hand wrapped around mine.

Creighton releases his hold on me slowly, but his eyes never leave mine. He's daring me to ask him the question that's burning on my tongue. So I do.

"You're staying?"

He doesn't answer right away, just continues to hold my gaze until the urge to fidget has me shifting where I stand.

"We're going to get one thing straight."

"Okay," I whisper.

"This whole disappearing act bullshit? It's not so much fun to be on the other end, is it?"

I knew there would be consequences for my actions. I break his stare, looking down at my feet. "No. It's not."

He drops my hand and raises it to my jaw. Tilting my chin up, he forces me to meet his eyes. "No, it's fucking not, Holly. And I'm done with it. No more running. This isn't a game."

My stomach flops wildly, and I know he's right. "Okay. No more running."

His grip on my chin tightens. "You have a problem, you feel the need to run, you come to me and we'll figure it out."

I nod, but instantly know he'll want the words. "Okay. I . . . I'll come to you. I won't run. I swear."

"Good girl." His touch turns soft, his thumb smoothing across my cheek.

"So you're staying?" I ask again, needing to hear those words from him.

"Yes, I'm staying."

"You're sure?"

He nods again, a smile tugging away the serious expression he had only moments ago. "Yes. Because you're here."

"As simple as that?"

"Not everything has to be complicated, Holly. *We* don't have to be complicated."

Creighton releases his hold on me, but his eyes never leave mine. I'm processing what just passed between us. I open my mouth to say something, but words desert me completely. Instead I reach into a bag on the table and start removing the contents. I freeze when I pull out a box of Lucky Charms.

Staring at the brightly colored cereal box, I mumble, "You bought Lucky Charms?"

"I thought you liked them. You mentioned them in your first single."

This time my stomach flops again, but it's a completely new emotion fueling it. My reference to the cereal was one fleeting mention in the second verse. Most people probably wouldn't really notice.

"You actually listened to the lyrics of my first single?"

Creighton straightens. "Holly, I've seen you perform live almost a dozen times. I know every word of every song at this point."

"Oh."

"Yeah. Oh." He turns, and instinctively I back up until my spine connects with the fridge.

He doesn't touch me, just presses a palm to the fridge on either side of my head.

"Why does that surprise you? It shouldn't."

"I just figured that . . ."

"What?"

"That you watch me but don't really pay attention. You've got more important things to think about."

He shakes his head. "You don't get it, Holly, and I'm not going anywhere until you do."

"Get what?"

"That you're the most important thing in my life now."

The box slips from my nerveless fingers and lands on the floor.

He smiles, but it's more predatory than anything else.

"See? You don't believe me. But you will."

My brain is trying to work. Trying—and failing.

Lifting a hand to my chin, Creighton tilts it up before lowering his mouth nearly to my lips. My breasts rise and fall, pressing against his chest, and my heart hammers against my ribs.

"Well, maybe your body believes me. I guess I'll start there and work my way into convincing the rest of you."

I expect him to crush his lips to mine, but he doesn't. He brushes them lightly over my lips, his tongue darting out, teasing, tasting . . . seducing.

My hands find their way to his upper arms and curl into the soft cotton of his shirt, sliding upward and testing the thick muscles of his shoulders. The sweet, soft kiss is driving me out of my ever-loving mind, when all I really want to do is climb the man like a dang coconut tree.

Not that I've ever climbed a coconut tree, but those guys on TV make it look so freaking easy and cool, and you get the prize when you get to the top, which in this case, would be my pussy against Crey's mouth, so that's pretty much the same thing, right?

My mind spins, my inner thoughts turning into a crazy ramble.

Screw it.

I hop up and wrap my legs around Crey's hips and practically attack him. I register the slight *umph* at the impact of my body slamming into his, and my legs attempt to squeeze the life out of him like some kind of anaconda, but I don't care. I want him. *Bad.* Right now.

Creighton's head moves back an inch, but my hands

are already tangling in his dark hair and fusing his lips to mine. I'm on the offensive here. I'm the aggressor. And it's *glorious.*

Because I know, deep down, I'm only in charge because he lets me. Which gives me a thought. I release his hair and pull my mouth away from his.

"How do you want to convince me? Because right now, I'd like you to *convince me* against the kitchen table."

Creighton's whole chest rumbles with his chuckle. "Jesus, woman. I fucking love you."

We both freeze, and the words seem to hang in the air between us.

"What did you say?" I whisper.

His jaw tenses, his stare intensifying. "I said I fucking love you."

It's not eloquent, it's not elegant, and it's definitely not fancy. It's raw and real and spur of the moment.

"Do you mean it?" I ask quietly.

His dark eyes spear straight to the heart of me, and he lifts a hand to cup my cheek again. "Of course I mean it. I rarely say anything I don't mean."

I open my mouth to say something . . . what, I'm not sure. But Creighton's thumb slides over my lips and he shakes his head.

"No. Don't say anything. When you tell me how you feel, I don't want there to be any hesitation, any question. I want the feeling to be burning through you so hot and fierce that you can't hold it back, and you blurt it out at the most inopportune moment. That's what I want from you, Holly. Until I can have that, I'll settle for the rest of you. Because that's a pretty fucking fabulous deal on my part too."

I'm pretty sure my insides just melted. Maybe my heart. Most definitely my panties.

I love that he wants the same raw, real, and beautiful declaration from me—and he's willing to wait for it.

"You're so getting laid right now."

His grin dang near stops my heart. "I know."

He turns and sits me on the kitchen table. Uncurling me from around his body, he scoops up all of the grocery bags, opens the fridge, and shoves them inside.

"Really? They don't all need to—"

"Do you really care right now?" Crey asks.

I shake my head. "Nope. Not even a little bit."

He slams the fridge door. "Good."

Only one step separates us, and I already have my shirt over my head and tossed to the floor by the time he closes that tiny distance.

Eager doesn't begin to cover how I'm feeling, and by the grin on Crey's face, he has no problem with my eagerness. Quite the opposite, judging by the bulge in his jeans. His eyes make a valiant attempt to stay on my face, but my heaving lungs have my boobs bouncing in my bra.

"Jesus Christ, Holly. You're fucking incredible."

I lean back on the table, my hands sliding across the weathered wood. Crey's hands find the button of my jeans and unsnap it, tugging the zipper down in one smooth motion before peeling them off my legs.

"Woman, I'm going to fuck you so hard we break this

goddamn table."

"Thank God," I whisper.

CHAPTER SIX

Creighton

Seeing Holly spread out on the table, eyes shining, tits heaving, and legs spread, almost stops my heart. Every fucking time. You'd think I'd be used to it by now. But there's something about her that grabs hold of me and won't let go.

I think it might be the universe telling me that I need to appreciate every fucking minute I have with her, because if I don't, a sorry bastard like me might have her snatched away before I know what happened. I've already learned what it's like to lose her—twice now—and that gut-wrenching emptiness isn't something I ever want to feel again. My heart is on the line here, which is completely new territory for me.

I drop to my knees between her legs, a hand on each

knee. Sliding my palms up her thighs, I say, "It's been too fucking long since I've had my mouth on your cunt."

Holly nods. "Yes. Yes, it has. I totally agree."

I'm going to fuck the sass right out of my sassy little wife. Well, maybe only most of it. I happen to like her sass. I reach up and grab the front of her lacy thong and rip it off.

"Hey!"

"Unless you're moaning or saying 'more' or 'harder' or 'yes' or 'like that' or 'Creighton, you're a fucking pussy-eating god,' I don't want to hear it, Holly."

I look up and catch her saucy grin.

This woman.

I wrap my hands around her thighs and yank her ass to the edge of the table. I don't wait any longer before lowering my mouth to her cunt.

I could eat Holly's pussy for every goddamn meal of the day. Using everything I've got—tongue, lips, teeth—I devour her until she's writhing on the table. I slide two fingers inside her just as she begins to clench and the orgasm rips through her.

The muscles of my jaw tense in anticipation. I want to feel that on my dick. I pull back, grab her hand, and put it on her pussy.

"Keep touching yourself. I want you coming again by the time I'm splitting you wide open with my cock."

Her eyes, already hazy, widen. But she complies, her hand landing on her clit and teasing and circling it in a way that prolongs her pleasure and has her hips bucking toward me.

I didn't think my dick could get any harder than it already was, but watching her play and keep herself on the edge holds a top spot on the list of the sexiest fucking things I've seen Holly do.

I rip open my jeans, grip my shaft, and line the head up with her entrance. "Hard and fast, yeah?"

She nods, her head jerking.

"Then let's get to breaking this fucking table."

I slam home, balls deep in one thrust, and Holly's scream of pleasure echoes in the small kitchen. Her pussy grips my cock and flutters, signaling the orgasm rippling through her.

"Jesus, woman."

I slide out and thrust again. Over and over and over again, almost mindlessly. With one hand braced on the shaking table and the other wrapped around her hip, I use my thumb to help her stroke her clit, adding more pressure and sending her into spirals of pleasure as orgasm after orgasm streak through her.

I've lost count when she finally grabs my hand with hers and stills it. Which is probably a good thing, because my balls are so high and tight, they're going to blow whether I want them to or not.

When I pump one last time, her inner muscles clench me so hard I can barely move. Then I let go, emptying myself inside her before twining her legs around me and lifting her up to my chest. Her head slumps against my shoulder, and we've taken two steps toward the stairs when the table groans.

And collapses.

Holly's soft giggle is one of the sweetest sounds I've ever heard in my life, and one I'll never get enough of.

Against her temple, I say, "No more running, Holly."

She pulls back and presses a kiss to my lips. "I promise."

CHAPTER SEVEN

Creighton

Other than my mother and my sister, I've never told a woman that I loved her. Yes, I know I've been married twice before Holly, and that makes me one cold bastard. But I don't say things I don't mean, and now that I've said the words to Holly, it means a hell of a lot more than if I said them before. Because before, they would have been a lie. I've never felt like this in my life. It's all her.

Now I just have to get her to believe that I mean it. Instinctively, I know my only choice is to show her.

Spending the day in bed may not seem like the most romantic way to get a woman to believe you're in love with her, but Holly and I haven't had time to just *be*. We've constantly been on the move since day one, and I want some time to just *be*. So that's exactly what we're going to do.

She looks at me like I've lost my mind when I tell her and settle us into her bed.

"We're going to what?"

"We're going to leave our cell phones downstairs, we're not answering the door, and unless the house is burning down around us, we're not leaving this room except to get food. And I might just feed you by hand."

She raises an eyebrow. "Are you serious? What about your empire?"

"It'll keep running without me."

Holly doesn't need to know that there are matters that undoubtedly require my attention, but right now, I don't care. I hire competent people for this very reason, and Cannon practically inhabits the business side of my brain. He knows what to do.

Even knowing that, before I wouldn't have dreamed of letting a day go by without at least checking in. But looking back now, it makes me realize all the more that I never had anything else in my life that was important enough to take me away from it all.

With Holly, I've dropped everything—more than once—to chase after her, and I'll do it again if I have to. My hope is that she'll never run again, however. Before we leave this town, she will understand that what I told her is true: she is the most important thing in my life. For no one else would I pull my focus this far from the business that I've built from nothing. But if I can't take time to enjoy what matters most to me, how successful am I, really?

I need to tell her about my acquisition of Homegrown, but I'd rather wait for another time. Although if anything will show her just how serious I am about her happiness, that might be it. Now she'll have the freedom to take the reins of her own career, and not be subject to the whims of the jackass record execs who don't have her best interests anywhere near the top of their priority lists.

But there's time to have that discussion later. Right now, I want to learn about the side of Holly I've never been privy to before. I want to know everything about her. Not one detail is too small.

"Tell me about what it was like to grow up here."

I've got her tucked against me with her head resting on my chest, and she freezes as soon as I ask my question.

I look down, my chin brushing her forehead. "Holly, I've seen the town; it's not a bad place. There's no reason to be ashamed."

Her hand, whether she's aware of it or not, curls into my side and pulls me closer. She says nothing.

"Holly?"

She mumbles something I can't make out.

"What was that?"

"You haven't seen where I really grew up, though."

"Is it far from here?"

She starts to pull away, but I tighten my grip around her, not willing to let her separate from me.

"No. I want to hold you."

I'm pretty sure it's the first time I've ever said those words to a woman, but it's also totally fucking true. I suspect that whatever Holly's about to say is something I don't really want to hear, because it's something that bothers her a lot. And if it bothers her, then it's going to bother me.

"I told you about my mama. We bounced from trailer to trailer in Rusty Meadows, which is a couple miles from here, across the river. It's called Happy Meadows, but no one actually calls it that."

"Was it an okay place?"

She shrugs against me. "The people were generally pretty nice, with the exception of the times the guy she'd shacked us up with would toss us out. Sometimes I'd come home from school and find my clothes in the dirt because Mama did something to piss the guy off. Usually messing around with someone else and getting ready to jump ship. She called it lining up her next opportunity. Everyone else called it being a cheating whore. The thing that sucks worst about living in a small town is that everyone assumed I was just like her."

I recall an offhand comment she made a couple of weeks ago about some boy offering her money for a blow job.

"But you set them straight."

"I just became an introvert. I didn't talk to anyone. Didn't date boys; didn't talk to boys. I didn't want to be like my mama. Didn't even have a boyfriend until I was a senior in high school. But she was gone for years by then. People started to forget about her, at least a little."

"Where'd she go?"

"She hitched her wagon to a man who could afford to keep her in style. He bought her a Cadillac Eldorado and they took off. I didn't see her again until *Country Dreams* happened, and now she just shows up when she needs money, which I don't really have."

"Until you married me and I sent her off on a fully paid vacation, and made myself into an easy target."

Holly sighs. "But you made her go away, and that's all I wanted."

I press a kiss to her forehead. "Are you going to take me to Rusty Meadows while we're here?" I'm not even really sure why I ask the question.

Holly shifts, and I think she's shaking her head. "No. It's not something I like to remember. This house," she jerks her chin toward the ceiling, "is the only home in this town I want to remember."

"Fair enough. And you were how old when you moved in?"

"Fourteen. Best thing that ever happened to me. Gran was friends with Ben and he gave me a job, which led to me singing karaoke and falling in love with being onstage, and the rest is history and would make a great country song." She pauses. "Speaking of which, I should totally write that one. I need a few more for the big-box exclusive tracks before I get back to Nashville."

She settles down on my chest again, and I can feel the tension drain out of her. Which is somewhat surprising, because now the subject of geography has come up. It's something that's been weighing on my mind, but it's not impossible. It'll just take some finesse.

I lean up on my elbow so I can see her face. "When do you need to be back in Nashville this time?"

"I need to be in the studio two weeks from tomorrow to cut the tracks, and I need to hammer the last few songs out with Vale once I've got ideas and practice them with the band. So probably . . . five or six days? Maybe sooner?" She glances up at me. "Is that going to be a problem?"

"No. We'll figure it out. You know there are recording studios in Manhattan, right?"

Her expression falls. "I . . . I just don't feel comfortable there. It's intimidating. Everyone's so focused and intense, and I feel like I'm just wandering around, hoping to hell I don't get lost. I don't mind feeling small in the grand scheme of things, but something about New York just makes me feel . . . inadequate. I know it's your place, and I'm not saying I won't go back and try to learn to like it, but I don't think I'm ever going to like it enough to want to live there permanently."

I can't say that her words don't disappoint me, because they do. I hate that she doesn't feel comfortable in the city that I love, but the fact that she's willing to try is a good sign. I'm not going to force her into something that clearly makes her so uneasy, but still, I think there's hope.

I press another kiss to her temple. "Next time, I'll show you a New Yorker's New York. The city has enough to offer that I think even you'll find something to enjoy. And I know it doesn't help to tell you that you belong there just as much as anyone else, but you do. Maybe more than anyone else, because you're mine. So if you're willing to give it another chance, I promise I'll give the entire city to you on a platter."

"Okay," she whispers.

I pull her against me tighter. "Thank you."

She snuggles against me, and I can't help but realize that this is the first time I've ever actually *cuddled* with a woman. It's nice. But I have a feeling it's only nice because it's Holly. She's turned my entire fucking world upside down, and it's the best goddamn thing that has ever happened to me.

My self-congratulatory thoughts falter when she asks, "Will you tell me about what it was like for you growing up? Since we're doing the sharing thing?"

My heart stutters as pangs of loss and grief stab through it. I swallow against the pain of old wounds never fully healed. Because do you ever fully recover from the loss of your parents? Especially when they're ripped from your life without warning?

I pause for the length of a few breaths before finally speaking. "Up until the age of ten, my childhood was simple. My parents were dedicated to serving others. They were missionaries. When I was six, we moved to Papua New Guinea. We lived there for four years. I don't remember a lot before that, to be honest. Everything there was so vivid and alive. Simple. Amazing. I ran wild with the other missionaries' kids, and the mothers took turns homeschooling us. It was basically the best childhood a kid could ask for. My sister was born there, about a year before . . . everything changed."

Holly's palm begins stroking up and down my chest, and I wonder if she knows she's soothing me. It's a very wifely gesture, and it gives me a shot of steadiness to continue. I haven't told this story in years, not since I told Cannon. Like I did then, I just have to recite the facts or I'll never get through it.

"Sometimes I feel bad that Greer was too young to remember any of those good days, but then again, she also doesn't remember any of the bad. Including the day trip I took with another missionary family, because my best friend James and I were dead set on seeing the tree kangaroos. His dad promised us that he'd find them for us, and he did. We came back late in the evening to the village, and found that fifteen people were slaughtered by a vigilante mob, including my parents, who tried to stop them. The mob was hunting down people accused of witchcraft. It seems insane in this day and age, like something out of the Salem witch trials, but it still happens there, even today."

"Oh my God," Holly said softly. "How did I not know about this? The press—how do they not—?" She left her question hanging, but I knew what she was asking.

"My uncle paid a lot of money early on to cover it up. It wasn't hard. News doesn't travel very quickly or efficiently from Papua New Guinea. I certainly don't tell people, and my aunt and uncle didn't want the notoriety. They were put out enough having to become responsible for two children they never wanted. They were the guardians my parents named in their will. I overheard James's father telling his mother that my uncle asked if the church could find someone else to take us."

"Oh my God."

My face twists into a grimace. "It's always good to know that you're not wanted."

Something wet hits my chest, and I glance down. Tears have gathered at the corners of Holly's eyes, and a few more splash onto my skin. I catch them on my thumbs.

"Sweetheart, don't cry. It's not worth it. Not at all."

"But you were only ten. And—"

"And you were only fourteen. If you think about it, we're not all that different. You got dropped off on your gran's front porch, and I got shipped off to boarding school. I'm just happy as hell that you had a grandmother who loved you, and my aunt fell in love with my little sister. Greer became the daughter she never knew she wanted."

Holly's smile is wobbly and utterly adorable, so I pull her up my chest so I can reach her lips with mine.

"I don't want you to cry for me. Neither of us can change our pasts, but somehow, all of these things happened in a way that made it possible for our paths to cross. No tears are necessary; I've got you in my arms, and I've never been happier in my life than I am right now."

She blinks, her eyes glassy with unshed tears. "Damn it, Crey. You can't say things like that if you don't want me to cry."

I frown. "Why?"

"Because it's not fair. And if you're trying to make sure I have no chance of holding on to any piece of my heart where you're concerned, you're doing a damn good job of that too."

My frown smooths into a small smile. "Under any other circumstances, I'd say I don't fight fair to get what I want. But when it comes to this, I want you to give it to me of your own free will. I'm not taking it by strategy, power play, or seduction. I want it because you want me to have it. Freely given. Earned. And that will be the most valuable thing I've ever received."

Her tears fall freely, dotting my face as she leans to kiss me. "Shut up and kiss me before I drown you with happy tears."

So I do. And then we do something else I've never done before.

We make love.

CHAPTER
EIGHT

Holly

*D*ress warm, he said. *We're going to be outside for a while.* That was it; no other explanation. And then he left the room.

The last two days have been surreal. So surreal that I'm going to give myself a legit bruise if I pinch myself one more time to make sure I'm not dreaming.

Yesterday we spent the entire day in bed, just like Crey said we were going to do. I lost track of the number of orgasms I had. My lady parts are actually sore today. Crey gave me a dark look when I winced as we got out of bed this morning.

"I need to take more care with you. No sex today. You need to recover."

"That's not fair!"

His dark look turned smoldering. "Doesn't mean I can't fuck that sassy little mouth of yours."

And *that's* all it took for my previously mentioned lady parts to perk up and claim they were in perfect working order. I tried to tempt him later, but he didn't take the bait.

I needed to get some songwriting done this morning, considering I have a deadline bearing down on me, so we retreated to our separate corners. Crey set up his laptop out in Gran's back room—the one that was added on to the house about sixty years prior, but never properly insulated. It was drafty, but he didn't seem to mind. I offered to share the repaired kitchen table with him, but he declined, saying he didn't want to interfere with my concentration because he had calls to make.

So instead, I spent most of the morning watching him through the window in the wall that separated the kitchen from the back room addition. Even in this little house in Kentucky, he looked all business. He stood and paced and shoved his fingers through his hair as he talked with his hands. It was fascinating to see him in full empire-running mode.

I was unable to concentrate on my own task, so I dropped my pencil and slipped into the back room and dropped to my knees in front of him, just as he lowered himself into an aging La-Z-Boy recliner.

His eyes dropped to mine questioningly, but he didn't stop me as I ran my palms up his thighs and reached for the button of his jeans.

He mouthed *what are you doing*, but I ignored him and unbuttoned and unzipped them. He didn't object overly much to my actions because he lifted his ass and let me tug his jeans down—and God love the man—because he nearly always went commando. I can't be the only woman in the world to think that is sexy.

He continued his call, but his answers shortened to single words—yes, no, fine—as I wrapped my hands around the base and lowered my head to run my tongue from root to tip before going in whole hog and deep throating him for the win.

I was in a go-big-or-go-home mood.

His choked-out, "Fuck. No, excuse me. Sorry. Wasn't talking to you," had me humming a little giggle around his cock.

After he muttered, "Please continue," Crey's hand found my hair and guided my movements. He slid into my mouth with long, sure strokes, and I took his cock all the way to the back of my throat with each thrust.

Ending the call with an abrupt and clipped, "We'll finish this later," he dropped the phone to the floor. It reminded me of the time I touched myself in front of him while he was on the phone in our hotel room back in San Antonio.

As soon as he dropped the phone, Crey cupped both my cheeks and tilted my face up at him. The look on his face was adoring.

"Best decision I ever made, Holly. Best decision I ever fucking made was making sure that missed connection went viral."

Tears stung my eyes, and not because of the cock hitting the back of my throat.

"I'm gonna come, sweetheart. You ready to swallow me down?"

I nodded, ready to take anything this man wanted to give me. Everything he wanted to give me.

Whoever says giving head can't be a romantic experience clearly isn't doing it right. I shiver at the memory. I don't know when things changed between us, exactly, but I know everything has. Hell, I don't even know when I started thinking of him as *Crey* instead of *Creighton*, but I do.

What's more, I trust him. And even bigger than that? I'm falling in love with him. I should be terrified, but instead, I'm excited.

Being back in Gran's house, it's easy to acknowledge that my future before *Country Dreams* was just a big yawning emptiness. And then after *Country Dreams*, it became some crazy, scary ride, one I could only do my best to hold on to and not get bucked off and land on my rear in the dirt like a bull rider who didn't make it the full eight.

Now, though, the future lies before me like an amazing adventure I can't wait to experience with this man at my side.

When I finish getting ready and step out of the bathroom, I expect to find Crey waiting in the bedroom, but instead I find a gift-wrapped package on the bed.

What the hell?

I study the box. It's about ten inches long, approximately the length of Crey's own package—not that I'm comparing—and eight inches wide and three inches tall. It's wrapped in simple brown craft paper and a turquoise ribbon.

I reach for it and pull my hand back. *Seriously, what the hell?*

"Open it."

I jump at Crey's voice coming from the doorway behind me, and spin to look at him.

"What's this for?"

"It's for you."

"But why?"

"Because."

He crosses his arms, and I can't help but drool a little over how his shoulders and chest look in the fitted cable-knit sweater he's wearing. The man shouldn't be allowed to go out in public looking so damn sexy. I need to cover him in Carhartt so the local ladies don't know what kind of exotic species of man they're missing out on. They'd mob him, and I'd have to cut a bitch.

"Open it," he says.

There's something ridiculously endearing about the simple wrapping. I carefully open the paper, because, not surprisingly, I don't get a lot of gifts. I want to cherish this one. This isn't like the racks of designer clothes he had some personal shopper pick out for me. No, this seems much more special.

It could be an owner's manual to the freaking rental car, and you wouldn't be able to wipe the smile off my face. I fold open the paper and still.

Keeper of Beautiful Songs

It's a leather journal, and the words are tooled in simple script on the front.

I blink back tears, lifting a hand to my mouth. "Oh my God. It's . . . it's beautiful."

Creighton crosses the room to stand beside me. "There was a woman at the grocery store selling them in a little stall in the front."

I squeeze my eyes shut, because I can picture Delores Maynard and her arthritic hands that can still take leatherworking tools and turn simple cowhide into beautiful pieces of art. The grocery store lets her set up her little stall so she can supplement her Social Security income and the tiny pension her husband left after he died in a mine collapse forty-odd years ago.

"You bought this yesterday?"

"Yes. That's why it took me a little longer than I planned. I knew you had to have it."

"Yesterday, when you still should've been pissed that I left New York—*again*—and you'd found me the night before hammered and out with another guy and—"

Crey holds up a hand to interrupt. "Yesterday, when I was trying to figure out how to show my wife that she means everything to me so I don't fuck this up and lose her for good."

That little piece of my heart I was holding on to? No longer mine.

I carefully lay the journal on the bed and stand to face him.

"When did things change? When did this go from being a whim to being . . . *everything*?"

Crey lifts a hand and brushes a flyaway strand of hair

out of my face. "I know I should have an answer for this that's epically romantic, but I don't think I can pinpoint the exact moment. I knew you were meant to be mine from that first night, but you're right—it was nothing but a gut feeling. I wanted you. Knew I had to have you. Wasn't going to stop until I found you."

When I smile up at him, he smiles back, but his expression sobers.

"Coming home to find you gone that first time made it clear to me that I had something to lose. Watching you onstage that first night in San Antonio made me realize that you weren't only a unique woman, but an extremely talented one that I would always have to share with the world, because it wouldn't be fair for me to keep you all to myself. I thought I would struggle with that, but instead, it's made me insanely proud to know that you're mine."

He pauses, jaw tensing. "The second time I came home to find you gone, I knew my heart had walked out the door. I don't ever want to feel like that again, Holly, and I'll do whatever it takes to make sure it never happens again."

His words stir up so many different emotions. I'm still trying to process them all as he pulls me out of the bedroom and down the stairs.

Surveying my outfit, he asks, "Are you sure you're going to be warm enough?"

"If you'd tell me what we're doing, it'd be easier for me to decide."

Crey grabs a flyer off the kitchen counter and holds it out to me.

DIRTY TOGETHER

GOLD HAVEN WINTERFEST

My eyes dart up to his. "Are you serious? You really want to go to this?"

"I have it on good authority from Delores Maynard that it's a good time. Not to be missed. Plus, she'd like to see you again. She was hoping for an autograph."

The fact that he chatted with the old woman while she made the journal makes me melt a little more.

I lean up and press a kiss to his lips. "Okay. Winterfest it is." A thought flashes through my brain. "But I forgot something. I'll be right back, and we can head out."

CHAPTER
NINE

Creighton

I'm about to pull out of the A&W parking lot, and I'm still amazed that we drove an hour to eat burgers and drink root-beer floats in the car.

I look sideways at Holly, who's grinning in the passenger seat. "I still can't believe you'd drive this far for fast food."

She reaches for the radio power button and tunes it to the local country station, which is no surprise.

"It's not like there was much else to do around here. We'd pool our money for gas and get out of town when someone had their parents' car. You could only eat so much Mr. Burger. Besides, A&W is the best. You can't get root beer like that just anywhere."

Her smile is infectious, and I lean over the center console to press a kiss to her lips before I back out and head in the direction of Gold Haven.

An hour later, I've learned a few things. First, Holly knows the lyrics to every damn country song on the radio. Second, listening to her attempt to sing bass notes is fucking adorable. And third, I need to come up with a foolproof way to calm my dick down, because she gets me harder than a rock without even trying.

The way she wiggles her ass in the seat and uses her fist as a microphone and belts out the songs . . . Jesus. I was tempted to pull the car over several times and fuck her senseless on the shoulder of the road. The only thing that stops me is knowing that she's likely still sore as hell from yesterday. I haven't missed her wincing this morning, and given how badly I want her, there's no way I'll be able to take it easy.

Since the main streets are blocked off for Winterfest, we pull onto one of the side streets. I still have no idea what Winterfest actually entails, but I see a big tent in the middle of the street and lots of outdoor heaters set up. I'm assuming there's beer involved, which isn't unwelcome.

Once we're parked, I'm out of the car and opening Holly's door before she can get out. She looks surprised. I shut the door behind her, lace my fingers through her gloved ones, and we head toward the revelry. As we get closer to the tent with lights strung from the sides, I see a bar and a band and a dance floor. Some people crowd around the bar while others are line dancing. The noise dies down a decibel or two when people catch sight of us.

"It seems we've been spotted," I say.

"Of course. You're hard to miss." Holly looks sideways at me.

"Me? I'm not the drop-dead sexy one here."

Her eyebrows go up. "I would argue that point. Do you see the drool dripping from those Cover Girl lips pouting at the bar?"

Not bothering to look in the direction she indicated, I stare down at her, hoping to make one thing very clear. "I don't see anyone but you, Holly." When she flushes pink, I squeeze her hand. "Care to dance?"

This time her eyebrows hit her hairline. "You know how to line dance?"

"Not even a little bit," I admit. "But I thought you could teach me."

She laughs, and I fight the urge to drag her out of the tent and back home to break another fucking table.

Holly twines her fingers in mine. "I'd be happy to school you in something, Mr. Karas," she drawls.

I lean down and speak directly into her ear. "You already did. In love."

She squeezes my hand and presses a kiss to my jaw. "That was cheesy as hell, and for the record, I loved it." She pulls me toward the dance floor just as the band announces they're taking a quick break.

"Well, hell. I guess we'll have to wait to teach you the Boot Scootin' Boogie."

"You really gonna get Karas out on the dance floor?" a familiar voice booms out.

When I look over my shoulder, I see Logan Brantley coming toward us with a beer in each hand.

I nod at his full load. "Double fisting tonight, Brant-ley?"

He shakes his head. "Nah. Was being polite and grabbed one for you, man. But if you don't want it, I know your wife likes a cold Bud just fine."

Holly shakes her head. "Oh no, I'm not drinking to-night. I may not ever drink again."

"An old pro like you? Damn, Holly."

"It's not like she's been able to drink for that long." I look down at my wife. "Unless you were a juvenile delin-quent."

Holly just shrugs. "There's not much else to do around here, I guess. Everyone looked the other way. Spent a lot of nights out in a field, chillin' on the tailgate of a truck backed up to a bonfire, stereo rockin' and a keg iced down in the bed." She laughs. "It sounds just like one of Boone's songs, probably because he writes from his experience just like I do."

Her expression turns wistful. "That's the best damn thing about country music. The heart and the truth. Writ-ing about things that real people can relate to because we live it. We sing about our lives and our roots and the heart of us." Holly shakes her head. "Now I'm sounding all mel-ancholy like I've been drinking. You better take that beer from Logan before I grab it."

I accept the beer, and Logan lifts his in a toast. "Cheers to the newlyweds."

We clink our bottles and I take a drink. It's not the fancy microbrew Cannon drinks, or my usual scotch or whiskey, but it's cold and delicious. The smile on Holly's face makes it taste even better.

"You better get in line for the food too, before that's all gone. You're almost too late as it is," Logan says.

"No need, we've already sampled the goodness of A&W this evening."

Logan looks sideways at me and Holly. "You let her drag you an hour away for burgers?"

"And cheese fries," Holly adds.

"You're a good man," Logan says, raising his bottle to his lips.

Holly shivers, and I release her hand in favor of wrapping my arm around her and pulling her into my side to keep her warm. It's probably an excuse, but I'd rather have her closer.

"Probably better than I deserve," Holly whispers.

I don't know what prompts her comment, but both Logan and I hear it and take issue with it.

"Now listen here—" he starts, but I interrupt.

"Not nearly good enough for you, if you ask me. But I'm working on it."

When the band comes back from their break and launches into an upbeat number, Logan motions with his beer.

"I'll leave you lovebirds to it. I got my eye on a likely lady for the night, and two-steppin' is a sure way to get her warmed up."

I don't turn to watch him leave because I've got my full attention on Holly. "You want to teach me to two-step, sweetheart?"

She smiles. "You want to?"

"I'm up for anything tonight."

Her smile turns a little mischievous. "Good to know. Finish your beer first."

We watch the couples gather on the dance floor, and Holly points out the general technique while I gulp down the cold beer. I haven't chugged like that since a frat party in college.

Once I finish, the song is just ending, but the band launches into another two-step number. We step onto the dance floor, and I've got one of Holly's gloved hands clasped in mine, and the other is on my shoulder. I pull her closer than is probably necessary, but I can't help but want to have her pressed against me. She's my woman, and it's my privilege to do so.

We're both aware of the random flashes coming from our periphery, but I don't fucking care if there are pictures all over the papers of us tomorrow. Holly is gazing up at me like I hung the moon. I never understood that saying before, but I feel like I finally get it now.

"Are you happy you came home?" I ask her.

Nodding, she replies, "Yeah, I am. And I'm happy you came too. I'm glad I don't feel like I have to hide this part of myself anymore, that I don't have to be ashamed of where I came from. It's a weight I've been carrying that I'm glad to be rid of."

"You never have to hide anything from me, Holly. I'm in love with the woman you are, and anything that made you this way is something to be grateful for."

Her cheeks flush. "You still haven't met my mama."

"We'll figure that out. There's got to be a way to smooth

it over and make that part of your life easier."

She shrugs. "I don't want to think about that tonight. Not at all."

"That's fine. What would you rather think about?"

Her smile comes back to life instantly, and once again, it's one that's colored with mischief. "Maybe the fact that I've got a surprise for you when we get home."

She already has my undivided attention, but now she's roused my curiosity as well. "Is that so?"

"Yep. One I think you're going to like."

I study her face as if I'll find the answer written there. The music is loud and the other couples are a few feet away, but still I pitch my voice low when I say, "You know I'm not lifting my ban on certain activities today . . ."

Holly leans in and up on her tiptoes, wrapping her arms around my neck, but continues to two-step. I'm proud that I've got the rhythm down well enough to lead at this point. But what she says next has me almost tripping over my feet.

"The giant butt plug in my ass says you don't need to lift your ban because you're going to be conquering new territory tonight."

Oh, fuck it. I sweep Holly off her feet and up into my arms. Several of the couples on the dance floor stop and the band quiets.

"Nothing to see here, folks. Just a man crazy in love with his bride."

And with that, I walk off the dance floor with Holly laughing against my chest.

"You're a menace," I say as I fight to keep the car on the road while Holly's clever little fingers work the buttons of my jeans.

"You announce to the whole damn town that you're crazy in love with your new bride, and you don't think you deserve road head for that? You're something else, Crey." Her hand slips inside my pants and closes around my dick.

"Jesus, woman."

I groan as she squeezes and pumps my cock. When she leans over the center console and the perfect heat of her mouth closes around the head, I breathe out her name.

She lifts up. "Just get us there in one piece, Crey. That's your job."

I don't look down, because if I do, there's a chance I won't be able to keep the car on the road. She wraps her fist around the base, and the flat of her tongue slicks up the bottom before she decides that mid-travel deep-throating is a good idea.

I white-knuckle the steering wheel and swallow back my groans. The woman is a cock-sucking goddess, and I mean that in the most complimentary way possible. Stroke after stroke with her tongue and the tight clasp of her lips wrapped around my shaft bring me close to the brink just before I flip on the turn signal to pull into the drive.

I debate whether I want to let go and come in her mouth, and then decide that if I'm going to be slipping inside that tight little ass of hers for the first time, maybe it's the practical thing to do.

Logic. Sure, let's call it that.

"I'm gonna come, baby. You ready for that?"

I slow the car to a stop in the driveway and slam it into PARK. Releasing the steering wheel, I bury my hands in Holly's hair. I feel her head bob, and I don't know if she's nodding that she's ready or if it's just her exuberant sucking. I open my mouth to ask again, but her hand cups my balls, and I lose my fucking mind.

"Holly—*fuuuck*."

The orgasm rips out of my balls and down her throat. *Jesus Fucking Christ.* This woman.

She sucks another stroke, cleaning me up, and I can't help but marvel at her. When she lifts her head, I brush her hair out of her face.

"You're amazing. And you're all fucking mine."

Her smile is sweet and beautiful, and I can't wait to get her upstairs. I rip open my door, round the hood, yank open hers, and reach inside. She squeals when I pull her out and toss her over my shoulder.

"Jesus, Crey. Did you even zip your jeans?"

I look down and become conscious of the draft that's very quickly freezing my dick. I shove my shit inside my pants. "No. Don't fucking care."

I stalk toward the door and then remember that I need keys. But Holly is already holding them out awkwardly around one side of my neck. I grab them from her.

"Good woman," I grunt out.

"You're just feeling good because you got a blow job in the car, and now you're going to brown town." She's giggling, and it's fucking contagious.

A deep chuckle works its way out of my lungs, and I can't remember laughing this hard in years. "God, you're good for me."

"And don't you forget it." She slaps my ass as I shove the key in the lock and open the door.

"Impossible."

CHAPTER TEN

Holly

The sound of Crey's laugh, coming easily and because of me, is up there on my list of favorite sounds. For some reason, it gives me the same kind of butterflies that hearing the host of *Country Dreams* announce my name as a finalist gave me. And it has nothing to do with the fact that I'm about to lose my anal virginity to something that's not silicone.

He heads straight for the stairs and jogs up them, holding me with one hand so I don't bounce with each step.

"Eager?" I ask, unable to hide the smile in my voice.

"When it comes to you, I'm always eager, Holly. That's something that's never going to change."

When he says things like that, my heart expands. He's

utterly convinced of the fact that we have a future together, and it's impossible not to believe in his conviction.

He carefully lowers me to the bed, and I have to smother a giggle of my own. His pants are barely half-zipped, and they're not covering the important parts.

"You could've taken the time to zip up, you know."

He cups my chin and tilts my head up to face him, pulling my gaze away from his crotch.

"Holly, when you told me that you had a butt plug up that sweet little ass of yours, I stopped caring about making sure my pants were zipped, because my dick knows exactly where it wants to be—and it's not in my pants."

"Oh my God, did you really just say that?" Sometimes his bluntness is more than I'm prepared for.

"It's the truth. And you're the one taunting me with the promise of that gorgeous ass."

I can't argue with that. "Still, you're crazy."

He stares down at me, his dark eyes flashing. "You make me crazy, woman. About you."

My giggle dies, and I swallow. "Is this for real?"

I can't hold the question back. I expect Crey to answer with a question of his own, like, *Is what for real?* But he doesn't.

"As real as it fucking gets, Holly. That's what I'm trying to show you. *This. Us.* It's as real as it fucking gets."

Creighton leans down and brushes his lips across mine, and I can't help but smile into his kiss. Who smiles into a kiss? Me, but only when I'm kissing this man.

He slants his mouth across mine, taking advantage of my parted lips, and his tongue dips inside, teasing and tasting. My hands skim up his sides of their own volition, trailing over the planes of muscles. Every inch of him is damn near perfect, right down to that dirty-talking mouth I can't get enough of.

When he finally pulls away, his eyes tell me everything he's thinking and feeling. Warmth spreads through me . . . and that's when it happens.

The words.

They bubble up, and I can't stop them. There's no holding them back.

"I love you, Crey."

His eyes, already soft, go even softer. "I feel like I've been waiting forever for you to say that."

"And I feel like I've been waiting forever for you, period. I should say there are so many things I'd do differently in my life, but I really wouldn't change a thing and run the risk of not ending up right here, right now, with you."

"You've changed everything for me, Holly. Every fucking thing."

I thread my hands through his hair, pull his mouth back down to mine, and kiss the ever-loving hell out of my man. Because he is mine. For the first time since we said "I do" in Vegas on New Year's Day, I feel like Creighton Karas is really mine. Body and mind. Heart and soul.

And I love him.

Our kiss seems to go on forever, each of us consuming the other. When Crey finally lifts his head, his cock is long and hard against my belly, and I'm reminded of exactly why we're here to begin with.

"I want you," I whisper.

"Are you sure?"

"Yes."

Crey pushes up to his knees and stares down at me. "Your heart and your virgin ass in one night. Jesus, Holly, I really am the luckiest fucking bastard on the planet."

I shake my head and laugh. "Seriously. Some of your lines tonight—not even a little bit smooth."

"I don't need to try to be smooth with you anymore," he says with a lopsided smile. "I can just be me."

Something pangs in the vicinity of the heart Crey just claimed as his, and I squeeze my eyes shut for a beat. I've officially been slayed. The player has dropped his game, and I've melted into a puddle on his bed.

"Let's get you out of those clothes, sweetheart."

I lift up my butt and let him peel my jeans, panties, and socks off me. My arms go over my head, and he tugs my sweater, long-sleeved shirt, and tank top off.

"I see you took me seriously when I told you to dress warm," Crey says, his tone wry.

"I'm starting to take everything you say seriously, I guess."

"Good." The single word carries a wealth of meaning.

I'm totally naked except for my bra, which I move to unhook, but Crey's hand stops me.

"Let me."

He strips me completely bare, which is probably an appropriate metaphor for what he's done all along. A lyric hits me at the worst possible moment, and I freeze.

Shit.

It's a good one. I can hear it.

Crey stills. "What's wrong?"

I bite my lip and look at him with his dick popping out of his jeans, rock hard. I'm completely naked, a butt plug up my ass.

Wow, Holly, marks for inconvenient timing.

"Holly, what the hell?"

"How pissed are you going to be if I call a time-out?"

Crey's eyes go wide. "A time-out?" The words come out slow and unsure. "What does that mean?"

I worry my lip between my teeth. "I need to write something down quick before I forget it."

I'm not sure what I expect, but it's not a brilliant smile, belly laugh, and Crey's head shaking.

"This is what I get for falling in love with a creative genius." He leans across the bed to grab the journal he bought me and holds it out.

I'm still reeling over the *falling in love with a creative genius* comment when he flips open the cover to reveal the pen clipped inside. I sit up, take the journal, and tug the pen out. Balancing it on my knee, I pause before I start writing. It almost seems like a crime to write in a journal so beautiful.

Crey doesn't miss my hesitation and correctly guesses the cause for it. "Sweetheart, she's making you another half dozen of them, so don't worry about it. Just write your lyrics."

Another rush of love sweeps through me, and I scribble for all I'm worth. Word after word, line after line. A song takes shape faster than one ever has before. I shut out the fact that I'm naked, but I don't shut out the fact that Crey is watching me. I pull creative energy from his presence, and it fuels me on.

I don't know if it's been five or fifteen or fifty minutes when I look up, but I suspect it's somewhere closer to my middle guess. If I'm right, I've never written a complete song so fast in my life. And it's a damn good song too.

The sight that greets me when I look up is also a complete shock—Crey, sitting on the edge of the bed with his hand wrapped around his cock, stroking it slowly, his eyes intent on me.

"Wha—what are you doing?" I stumble over my words, not because I'm the type to stutter, but because I'm so freaking shocked to see him jacking off to the sight of my naked songwriting.

"That was one of the hottest fucking things I've ever seen," he says.

"Are you serious?"

"Dead serious. And if you don't want me in your ass in the next five minutes, I'm going to be jacking myself off all over those lush tits of yours. Which, by the way, bounce a whole fuck of a lot while you're humming to yourself and scribbling away. If I hadn't just come down your throat, I might've accidentally shot my load all over your bed."

Oh my God. My shock at his words must show on my face because he keeps talking.

"I can't help that you're so fucking sexy, Holly. That's on you, my beautiful wife. So, what's it going to be?"

I try and fail at smothering my smile, because he's such a damn *man.* My skin prickles with nervous energy as I consider what we're about to do. I've been anxiously awaiting this moment since the first time Crey introduced me to the forbidden pleasures of my no-go zone.

Setting the journal aside, I meet his gaze. "I think I'm ready."

Crey's eyes darken with heat. "Good girl. Now come here. I want you."

I scoot across the bed toward him until I'm within reach. "How do you want me?"

"So perfect." His hands wrap around my waist and he turns me around so I'm on my knees, ass facing him. He trails the fingers of one hand up my spine. "I had some kind of crazy luck guiding me on Christmas Eve . . . I can't imagine having missed you that night. It would've been the biggest loss of my life, and I never would've had any idea what I'd missed out on."

He's already slayed me tonight with his words once, and I'm not sure I can handle more sweet Crey. It's a side of him I never expected.

"I'll never understand how it worked out the way it did, but I'm not about to question fate."

His fingertips skate back down, tracing the same path, leaving goose bumps in their wake.

"I never believed in fate until I met you. Now there's no way I'd believe this was anything but."

Shivers ripple through me, and I close my eyes and give myself over to the sensations—give myself over to Crey.

"Are you sure you want this? Because if you're not ready, I'm not going to push this on you." He pauses on the base of my spine, right above the crack of my ass.

I nod, but realize that it's just as important for me to say the words as it is for him to hear them. "I'm ready. I want you. I want this to be yours."

"If it ever gets to be too much, all you have to say is stop."

"I trust you."

He rises. "Now, where's the lube you secreted away in your bag with that sexy plug?"

"Bathroom counter."

I peek over my shoulder in time to catch his smile as he turns to head to the tiny bathroom.

When he comes back into the bedroom, he has the lube in one hand, and he's completely naked.

"I guess you really are eager," I say.

"When I'm about to sink into that perfect ass of yours? Even more so."

The ass in question bounces with my laughter.

"Then you better get over here and get to it."

My words are cocky and bold, but inside I'm fighting back tiny shivers of fear. It's not that I don't want to do this—I do. But there's something about the unknown, and I'm a little terrified that I won't like it, which will disappoint him. It's the same old self-doubt creeping up and chipping away at my self-confidence.

Crey must see something in my expression, because he pauses beside the bed. "Holly?"

I decide that voicing my fears is the best choice here. "What if I hate it? What if it's horrible?"

His expression falls for only a moment before the edges of his mouth curl up into a devastating smile.

"Then I'll give you all the orgasms you can handle another way."

"Are you sure? You won't care if I change my mind?"

The smile softens into something adoring. "Holly, all that matters is that I'm here with you, and you're enjoying what we're doing. If you want me to drop this lube, pull that plug out of your ass, and go find a game of Scrabble, I'll still be the happiest guy in this whole town."

The lump in my throat melts away, and I shake my head. "Let's leave the Scrabble for later. I'm ready."

Crey sits on the edge of the bed and strokes my back, kissing my neck before scraping his teeth along my ear. I shiver, and this time there is no fear involved. My nipples pucker almost painfully, and my pussy clenches. I'm achingly aware that it's empty. He finds the base of the plug and presses inward, lighting up my nerve endings in the most delicious way. A beat later and he's pulling it out.

He moves quickly, and I hear the top of the lube snap open before cool liquid dribbles down my crack. Goose bumps rise along every inch of my skin, and I squeeze my thighs together. His finger circles my ass, and I revel in the sensation. We've done this before, but knowing we're going all the way this time adds another layer of the forbidden.

When he slides it inside, I moan into the pillow beneath me. He moves it in and out, fucking me slowly.

"Goddamn, this is going to be amazing. I've thought about what it'd be like to have you beneath me just like this."

He removes his hand, and once again I hear the cap

on the lube. The next thing I feel is the nudge of the head of Crey's cock against my asshole. It's bigger than the plug, and I hope my preparation was enough.

"Ready, sweetheart?"

"Yes." There is no hesitation in my voice, because I know this is exactly what I want. Him, however he wants me.

He begins to push inside, and there's a twinge of pain, but the pleasure overwhelms it. I arch into him, pushing back, inviting him in farther. I want more. I need more.

"Jesus, Holly. You're so fucking tight."

He slides in the last few inches until he's seated all the way to the base. I shift my hips back again, pressing harder against him, and he reaches around my hip to find my clit. With two fingers teasing me, he slowly pulls out and begins to thrust.

Every movement triggers a new landslide of sensation within me. Pleasure ripples and squeezes and pulses through my body.

"Oh my God," I whisper as Crey pinches my clit between two fingers and tugs, all while picking up the pace of his thrusts.

The more he plays with my clit, the faster he fucks, and my need drives higher and higher. He responds by giving me everything I need but didn't know I needed before I can even think to voice it.

My mind seems to fracture under the onslaught of pleasure. Thoughts are impossible to grasp, not that I even want to think right now. I just want to feel. Which is good, because all I'm capable of is experiencing sensations.

And the sensation bearing down on me is a giant mother of an orgasm.

"Holy. Shit," I scream, my voice breaking as I come apart and my arms collapse.

Crey keeps thrusting. Once. Twice. Three more times. And then the sound of my name coming off his lips echoes in the small room.

He drops but catches himself before he crushes me on the bed. The frame creaks beneath us, and we both freeze.

"Oh sh—" Crey doesn't even get the word out before the bed collapses and we land with a thud as the mattress connects with the floor.

"Holy crap. And you didn't even plan to screw me so hard we'd break my poor Jenny Lind bed."

"Jenny who?" Crey asks, carefully pushing himself up off me, and reaching for a towel I didn't notice earlier.

He pulls out of my body and I immediately feel the loss of him. The fullness was intense and amazing. He crouches down and cleans me up while I lay on the mattress, still boneless and unwilling to move, despite the destruction of the furniture.

"Jenny Lind. It was an antique. It was Gran's bed when she was a girl. It was one of the few pieces I probably would have kept."

"We'll get it repaired. It's no problem."

I nod because he's right. It really isn't a problem.

"We're just breaking furniture right and left. Going to have to make sure whatever we buy for our new place is sturdy," Crey says.

I look sideways at him. "Our new place?"

"I think we need to buy a place in Nashville so we can have a home base there. We'll keep my place in New York, and figure out something that works for both of us. As much as you don't like the city, I do need to spend some time there. There are certain things I can do remotely, but I'm a hell of a lot more intimidating in person, and sometimes I need to throw my weight around to get shit done."

Warmth fills my chest that he's no longer dictating, but considering what's best for me as well. "Thank you for trying to figure this out."

He crouches again next to the bed. "I'd figure out how to move mountains for you, Holly."

I close my eyes briefly before meeting his again. "I think I'm finally getting that."

I reach for the blanket that's scrunched up beside me, and flip around so I'm sitting on my butt before I pull it around me.

"Now, how do you feel about Dirty Scrabble?"

CHAPTER
ELEVEN

Creighton

My stomach aches from laughing so hard, and I think it's safe to say I've never felt that kind of ache before.

"C-U-N-T. Cunt. Triple-word score. Eighteen points." Holly looks up at me, her eyes shining with what can only be called mirth. "I'm going to catch you. Fellatio as a double word was only four points more."

"Sorry, sweetheart." I shake my head, grinning as I lift my tiles and lay them on the board. "S-U-C-K-E-D. Another triple word." I mentally calculate. "Thirty-nine points."

"Damn it."

Holly's hands go to her hips, and she drops the blanket she had wrapped around her shoulders. My eyebrows shoot up because now I get to see her in her full naked glory.

She gives me a mock frown. "Why is it that every other freaking word you have is about dick sucking?"

I rest my hand over my abs as they clench again as another chuckle escapes. "Because I'm a guy. That's what I think about. Not too hard to figure out here. Let's not sugarcoat it—if I'm looking at your mouth, there's a decent chance I'm thinking about putting my dick in it. If I'm looking at your tits, there's a good chance I'm thinking about sucking on them or fucking them. Same with your pussy and your ass. Men are not that complicated."

Her chin juts up another inch. "I beg to differ. You're all sorts of complicated, Karas."

"I just like you to think that, Holly."

Her lips purse, and her eyes drop to her new tiles. The way *her* mind works fascinates me. The way she takes a flash of inspiration and turns it into a song . . . it's nothing short of amazing. Her lips spread into a triumphant smile, kicking up my anticipation a notch. The woman only needs to breathe, and I'm eager for whatever she's going to do next.

"D-I-L-D-O. Dildo. Seven points." She looks up. "You know, I've never actually owned a dildo. Or a vibrator. Whatever."

"Seriously?" The shock in my voice can't be missed.

"Well, no. I mean, yes, seriously. I've never owned one."

"How is that possible?"

"I just never went out and got one. I don't know. I figured my hand got the job done just fine."

I just shake my head at her confession. "I swear, everything that comes out of your mouth surprises me."

After a beat of studying her face, I look down at the tiles on my rack. I don't have many options. I decide on a word that's not all that dirty, but deem it appropriate nonetheless.

"M-I-N-E. Mine."

Holly looks at me strangely. "It's Dirty Scrabble, Crey. Not whatever-word-you-want Scrabble."

"True, but that's what you are, dirty or not, so that's my last word on the subject."

With that, I shove the game board aside, sending the tiles and racks flying, and pin her to the mattress.

Against her lips, I whisper, "I'll make my dirty contribution this way instead."

CHAPTER
TWELVE

Holly

I make my way down the stairs the next morning wearing only Crey's shirt, a pair of knee-high socks, and no panties. My plan is to oh-so-carefully bend over the counter and tease Crey with a flash of my goods, and tempt him into giving me what I want.

Last night after he scattered my Scrabble pieces everywhere, he was totally dirty, taking my ass again with his fingers—and his tongue—but refusing to take my pussy because he claimed it still needed another day of rest.

I'm bound and determined that's going to change today. But my plan is derailed when I overhear Crey talking in the back room through the partially closed door.

"I don't think you understand, Cannon, *this* is more important. *Holly* is more important. I know that you're—I

101

know. I know. But you're not listening to me." Crey turns his head and catches sight of me. "I'll call you back later."

He must not even listen for a reply because he drops the phone almost instantly and shoves the door open.

"Hey, you're up. How'd you sleep on our floor mattress? I still can't believe we broke the bed." His eyes dart to the repaired table. "And the table."

"Crey, what's wrong?"

His body language is off. His brow is creased and his jaw is tight, his demeanor at odds with his lighthearted words.

He shoves a hand through his hair and sighs, his lips turning down into a frown. "You know how I said sometimes I'm needed to show up and be intimidating in person and throw my weight around? Now is one of those times. I need to be back in New York."

Reality. That's what sucked the easiness out of Creighton's mood.

It wouldn't be realistic for me to think that we could stay in this little bubble forever. My time is slipping away too. If this is going to work, then we both have to attend to our lives.

"Then you should get back to New York and throw your weight around," I tell him.

His face is set, without a hint of a smile anywhere in his expression. "I told you I'd stay until you understood that nothing is more important than you, and if I leave, then I'm not doing that."

Once again, warmth spreads through me, and I shake my head as I lay a hand on his arm. "You've already shown me that. I believe you. Now go back to New York and take care of business like the ruthless guy I know you want to unleash."

A little of the tension drains out of his posture. "You're sure?"

"Yes. You told me this is as real as it gets, and real means that we each handle our own shit with the support of the other beside or behind us, whatever the case may be. If I can be with you, I will, and vice versa. We'll figure it out."

Crey leans down and brushes a kiss along my jaw. "I love you, Holly."

"Then go conquer the world. I'll be waiting for you when you get done."

He lifts his head and stares down at me, his eyes intent, and so much emotion shining in them. The force of it hits me in my chest.

"I thought I had everything," he says in a low voice. "And then I met you. Now I do."

I swallow, determined not to let the tears burning the back of my eyes free. "You can't say things like that. I'm seriously not equipped to handle it."

"I didn't know I was equipped to say things like that until you either. Guess we're both going to have to find our footing here."

Nodding, I squeeze his arm. "Get your stuff packed, and I'll drive you to the airport. I guess I should ask if you mind if I keep the rental car and take it back to Nashville."

He covers my hand with his. "Of course I don't mind. As long as you don't mind that you're getting a new car whether you want one or not. And I'm picking it out, since apparently your last two were Pontiacs, and Detroit doesn't even make those anymore."

"Whatever. Just know that I'm still gonna drive like a girl from Gold Haven, so you better get good insurance."

Under his breath, he murmurs, "On second thought, I'm buying you a tank."

I just laugh. I don't honestly care what he buys me. As long as it has four wheels and gets me from A to B. If it's too outrageously expensive, I'll bitch . . . and maybe concede gracefully.

Now that we've stepped into this new version of us, how he chooses to spend his money doesn't rub me the wrong way at every turn. Creighton doesn't need to buy me—he already has me. Now I think he's trying to cherish me and take care of me, which is something altogether different, and I'm not going to throw it back in his face.

"When are you heading back?" he asks.

Shrugging, I flip through my mental schedule, considering I don't have my phone at hand. "Probably not for another day or two. I've got some time."

I glance around the quiet room. "This has actually been exactly what I needed. I'm going to stay, fine-tune the songs as much as I can before I head back. I might even try to pack some stuff in my room and make a trip to Goodwill. I need to make a decision about the house."

"What decision do you want to make?"

"I should sell it. I have no earthly reason to keep it."

"But?"

"But I'm just not quite ready yet."

"Holly." Crey lifts his hand to my face. "You don't ever have to sell if you don't want to."

"It seems silly to keep paying the property taxes and utilities when no one lives here."

"Baby," he says, his eyes soft. "We can afford it."

"Okay, I won't sell it for now. It's nice to have somewhere to come home to. Besides, I'm finding that I like keeping a tie to my roots."

"Good. I'm glad." His phone buzzes in his hand, and Cannon's name flashes across the screen. "I need to take this."

"Go conquer the world from New York, Crey. We're going to be just fine."

I shove him toward the stairs, and he goes. Beyond his clipped greeting, I hear nothing of their conversation. Instinct tells me that all is not well back in New York at Karas International.

The urge to ask is strong, but I fight it back . . . now, and the whole drive to the airport. I'm still fighting it when Creighton cups my face and kisses the hell out of me, and when he climbs on the jet and gives me one final wave.

Alone in the Cadillac, I wonder if I shouldn't have fought the urge to ask.

CHAPTER
THIRTEEN

Holly

The next day, I've just scarfed down a tuna sandwich for lunch when someone knocks at the door.

Really? Again?

I've already received two deliveries from Crey today. First, Delores Maynard's grandson, Leander, dropped by with the other journals that Crey asked her to make for me. After I fished out a twenty to tip him, I almost swooned at the beautiful colors.

After that came Ben from Brews and Balls.

"What the hell are you doing here?" I asked him.

He hefted a black-and-pink bowling bag up with the hand not wrapped around his cane. "Special delivery from your man."

"What the hell?" I took the bag from him and unzipped it. A hot-pink glitter-swirled bowling ball with my name engraved on it sat inside, along with black-and-pink bowling shoes.

What in the world?

"Okay, well. Now that that's done, I gotta run, sugar. I'll see you at the lanes tonight, if you're coming in."

I mumbled something to him as he picked his way down the steps and shuffled to his car. I had no idea what I said, because I was too stunned. I pulled out the note stuck to the ball and set the bag on the floor.

Read me.

I tear it open and read it.

In case you get bored. Also, I think the citizens of Gold Haven would love to have a reason to get you back into the bowling alley to give another impromptu concert. I might have only caught the tail end of the last one, and even tequila spiked, it was amazing.
I miss you.
Yours,
Crey

Hell.

If I hadn't already given the man my heart, he would have stolen it right there over a pink glittery bowling bowl and black-and-pink bowling shoes. I may be the only woman on the planet to prefer this gift to a Harry Winston diamond collar, but there was more thought and effort tied up in this gesture, and that makes all the difference in the world to me.

The next knock on the door—which has morphed into angry hammering—jars me out of the memory.

"I'm coming, I'm coming," I mutter as I yank the door open.

I should have looked through the lace curtain covering the tiny window in the door. But I didn't.

"Hey, baby! Mama's home!"

CHAPTER FOURTEEN

Creighton

I hit the ground running when I arrived yesterday in New York, and have barely stopped since. Cannon scowled at me the entire time I was on the phone with Ben to get the bowling ball, shoes, and bag set up for Holly, but I kicked his ass out of the room when I arranged for the other delivery. That was the only time I spent on anything unrelated to business since I got here. Otherwise, it's been clusterfuck after clusterfuck.

My uncle is accusing me of breaching my duty of loyalty to my own fucking company, and usurping a corporate opportunity because I didn't allow the board of directors to vote on the purchase of Homegrown Records before I bought it personally.

I've spent almost every minute since I got here locked

in with my lawyers—the ones I had to hire personally to defend me since my company attorneys have a conflict of interest—and what they're telling me isn't good. Sure, there are plenty of arguments in my favor, good ones, but the fact that they're saying he has a case at all burns me straight to the gut.

There wouldn't be an issue if I'd put the matter on the agenda to be voted on, gotten the blessing of the board, and then proceeded with the purchase, but I was in such a goddamn hurry—so eager to do the deal for Holly and make sure the record execs couldn't screw her over—that I fucked up. I've never fucked up like this before. If my uncle files suit, my reputation in the business world, and with my own board and shareholders, will be damaged, maybe irrevocably.

I should have told Holly everything before I left Kentucky yesterday. She's the one person I want to vent everything to, and she's completely unavailable to me because I didn't open my fucking mouth and say word one about what I did.

I know it's because part of me doesn't want to tip the new balance we found. This harmony feels so fucking good, I don't want to screw it up before we even have a chance to enjoy it.

But this isn't something I want to tell her when she's not within my reach. I don't think she'll run again, but there's always the chance she may think I was trying to buy her, and I'm not taking the chance that this announcement isn't delivered with care.

What Cannon told me on the phone early yesterday

when he called me in Kentucky was only that my uncle planned to file suit—not that he has any actual grounds. I figured the lawyers would sort that shit out in record time. God knows I pay them enough. But no solutions yet. Just multiple possible courses of action qualified a dozen ways to Sunday.

I pick up my phone to call Holly anyway. Just hearing her voice will be an improvement.

Cannon's in the conference room next door when I pick up my phone and find Holly's contact—not that it's hard to find since it's number one in my favorites. Maybe that's why Cannon's been pissy lately. He knows he's been displaced.

It rings twice before she picks up.

"Crey?"

Relief slides through me at the sound of her voice. "Hey, baby."

"Hi. Can I call you back? I'm sort of . . . busy at the moment."

I hear voices in the background, and she must have her hand over the phone because I hear her shushing someone in a muted tone. The relief I feel fades.

"Holly? Is everything okay?"

"It's fine. Everything's fine. Can I call you back in a couple hours?"

Her voice sounds strained, and there's no way I believe her *everything's fine* line.

"Something's wrong. What is it?" I demand.

"I can't really talk now, but I'll tell you later."

I force down the urge to push her to tell me what the

hell is going on. "Call me anytime. I love you, Holly."

"'Bye, Crey."

She hangs up, and it isn't lost on me that she doesn't say she loves me back.

I'm not sure why I'm here, but for some reason, when I left my lawyers' office, I walked to the Rose Club at the Plaza instead of back to my penthouse. I shrug off my overcoat and hang it on the back of the velvet bar stool.

When the bartender heads my way immediately, which isn't surprising because the service here is impeccable, I say, "Bushmills 21, please. Three fingers."

"Yes, sir."

He moves away, reaching for the bottle and a glass, and I ease onto the stool and think about the last time I was here. Jesus, fuck. So much has happened since then.

The night I met Holly, I was sitting on one of the low couches in the corner, avoiding all human interaction, and most certainly avoiding a family dinner that would turn into my uncle berating me for every single goddamn thing I've ever done in my life.

Christmas Eve a year ago, after my sister begged, I agreed to go to my aunt and uncle's and pretend to be a family. Over perfectly cooked duck and way more scotch than he should be allowed to imbibe, my uncle unleashed a tirade about my ineptitude at business before shifting to highlight the failures in my personal life.

The final straw was his muttered comment about the

indignity of having to share a last name with me. My aunt blanched, but rather than wade into the fray, she only reached for another glass of wine. Even when I was a kid, she never said a word against my uncle.

I stood, apologized to my sister for being unable to keep up the pretense of family, and walked out.

This past Christmas, I refused to attempt the mockery of a family holiday again. Holly was the cure to my boredom, and to the thoughts of my less-than-ideal family situation.

When the bartender slides my drink across the smooth wood, I wrap my fingers around the glass and move away from the bar. As I settle back into my corner, I smile as the memory of Holly strutting into the bar floods my mind.

Damn. She looked just as gorgeous as she looked out of place. Short skirt, jacket too thin to possibly keep her warm, and cowboy boots. She tossed her wild mane over her shoulder, which I now know is from her crazy stage hair, and scanned the bar like she owned it. Even as her clothes screamed *I don't belong*, her attitude yelled *But I don't care*. It was that attempt at confidence and bravado that captured me first.

Well, that's a lie. It was her sexy-as-hell hair, lush tits, and perfectly rounded ass—and *then* it was her forged confidence with the underlying hint of vulnerability.

Everything about her, even the way she stood, threw out the vibe that she was trying to be strong but needed an even stronger hand to guide her. When I saw another man move in to take a shot, I acted without thinking—something I rarely, if ever, did before her.

I stalked over and claimed her as mine.

I can still remember, almost verbatim, what she said when she finally threw down her proposition after all the innuendos and flirting.

"I came here to find a hot guy who looked like he could handle himself, and see where the night takes us."

I mean, really, what does a man say to that except grab her by the hand and drag her back up to her hotel room? Because that's exactly what I did.

The memory slips away when a shadow falls onto the purplish-blue color of the light on the table in front of me. I look up to find Greer.

"Don't they keep you chained to your desk until midnight every night?" I ask with a smirk.

My sister's smile doesn't stretch as far across her face as it used to. She looks at her watch. "I know, right? Hell, Crey, I haven't gotten out this early in months. And it's all because I can't work on the project you've got everyone else locked down on. Sometimes conflicts of interest are a wonderful thing."

I check my watch and hate the fact that my little sister thinks that getting out of work at eight thirty is early.

"You don't need that job, Gree." The nickname is one left over from the little pieces of her childhood I got to witness during breaks from boarding school.

She rolls her eyes, drops her briefcase on the floor, and plops into the seat across from me. "I'm not living off your money. Besides, it's not like I'm going to be at the sweatshop forever. A few years will be enough to get me a job in-house, and then I'll be living the dream."

I think of the legal department at Karas International and how hard they're always working. "You realize the grass isn't always greener, right?"

"Don't burst my bubble just yet. I spent three years busting my ass for this degree; I'm going to use it."

I open my mouth to say something else, but instead of wasting my breath, I take another sip of scotch.

A server comes by, and Greer orders a gin and tonic.

"When did you switch to hard liquor?" I ask, the big brother in me coming out. "You used to drink wine, not gin."

The eye rolling commences again. "Calm down, Crey. I'm splurging on the good stuff because you're buying. Besides, Tristan is trying to get me to drink more 'sophisticated' drinks than just wine."

I frown at the mention of her boyfriend. "Tristan's a dick, Greer."

She glares at me. "He's not a dick. He's a good guy, really." By her tone, I'm not sure if she's trying to convince me or herself.

"Really? Then why aren't you with Tristan right now rather than your big brother?"

Her gaze drops and the glare fades away. "Because he doesn't like me coming over late. Says it messes with his sleep schedule. But we're going away together next weekend. We need some time alone to reconnect."

If Greer were any woman but my sister, I'd tell her that any man deserving of the title shouldn't care what time his woman is crawling into his bed. He should be happy as fuck she's there to *mess with his sleep schedule*. But I'm not going anywhere near the topic of sex with my sister. It's not happening. Not fucking ever.

Greer thankfully changes the subject. "So, when am I going to get to meet your wife?"

I think about the phone call that wasn't really even a phone call that Holly and I had earlier. "Soon. You should come to one of her shows. She's fucking amazing, Gree. You'll be absolutely stunned."

"Um, news flash, Crey. I've seen her perform on TV; I know what she sounds like. And you're right—she is fucking amazing."

"When did you see her on TV?"

"I watched the back episodes of *Country Dreams* as soon as your news hit the papers. I wanted to see this girl who's now my sister. You did good. She's crazy talented. They polished her up a lot from that first audition, but her voice has carried through. The judges were stunned."

I pull out my phone to call Cannon.

"What are you doing?" Greer asks.

"I'm getting a copy of that season of the show."

"You haven't already? Seriously? I thought that would've been in the background check."

"If it was, then Cannon didn't share it with me. Shit."

I don't know why I didn't do it sooner. My need to see the pre-famous Holly grows exponentially with each ring of Cannon's phone.

"Not a good time, Crey," Cannon says, his voice rough.

"Jesus, Cannon. If you're fucking someone, don't answer the goddamn phone then."

"We're in DEFCON 5 right now, so I figured it had to

be important. If it's not, I'll get back to Rachel, and we can discuss this in the morning."

"Guess I'm impressed you actually know her name. And yeah, it's important, but you can finish up with *Rachel* first. I want the season of *Country Dreams* that Holly starred on."

"You interrupted me for that?"

"It's important," I say, my tone clipped and no bullshit.

"And you already have it in your e-mail. Go look for my e-mail from New Year's Day, after you told me her name. I compiled the report and sent you everything."

"Thanks. Enjoy your night," I reply, and hang up.

Greer is grinning. "Told you."

"Did you listen to the whole damn conversation?"

"Hard not to."

I shake my head. "I need to get home. I've got some TV to watch." I lift my glass and down the rest of the liquor.

"Fine, leave your little sister to drink alone."

The server was just returning with her G&T. I pull out my wallet and toss a hundred on the table before grabbing Greer's hand and pulling her out of the chair.

"You're not drinking tonight. You're going home and getting a decent night's sleep before you go back to the office."

"I don't think so, Crey. I'm going to sit down, relax, and enjoy my drink. You run along and watch your wife before she was your wife. I'll see you in the morning. I'll be the one running around with partners snapping orders at me."

"At least tell me you're taking a cab home and not walking."

"It's like six blocks. Cab not required."

I sit back down. "I guess I'm waiting until you finish your drink then."

After walking my sister to her door, I walk back to my place. As soon as I'm in the door of my penthouse, I head for the office and pull out my laptop. It only takes a few minutes to dig through my e-mails and pull up the one that Cannon sent.

I start with the audition episode. To say I'm entranced would be an understatement.

I marvel at the roundness in Holly's face that she's since lost, and the polish that seems to smooth over her with every episode. I feel like I'm watching the making of a star, but the part that bothers me most? They didn't need to change a damn thing about her, because she was perfect from the moment she stepped onstage. Pink plaid shirt, jeans worn by time and wear rather than a designer's dictates, a pair of battered cowboy boots, and the biggest smile I've ever seen on her face.

I won't rest until I put that smile on her face again.

CHAPTER
FIFTEEN

Holly

Today is surreal. Not surreal in the way it was to stand on the stage of the Grand Ole Opry and perform, but still surreal all the same. If you were to google the definition of surreal, the Wickman mother-daughter heart-to-heart should pop up.

Mama showing up, all tanned, buffed, and polished from her vacation, isn't something I expected . . . but I guess I should have. After she called me from jail, I knew she didn't have a man in her life, although that's a situation that doesn't generally last long.

My bullshit detector immediately springs to life when she hugs me and says it's good to see me looking so happy.

Is this really my mother?

I'm so stunned and amazed that she wants to talk and

find out how I'm doing—and not about how much money I can get my hands on—that I practically hang up on Crey when he calls. But the fact that she hasn't mentioned a single thing about walking away with Gran's jewelry the last time she was here reminds me that she still is my mother, and puts me on the defensive.

When I set aside my phone, she says, "You could've talked to him, you know. You must miss him like crazy, being that he's not here and you're newlyweds still."

"Uh, I'll catch up with him later."

"If you're sure." She looks around the kitchen. "How about I make us some sweet tea and we can sit and talk a spell? I'm planning to head over to B&B tonight to catch up with some friends."

Ah. That sounds more like Mama.

"Okay."

I don't think I've ever turned down sweet tea, and I'm not about to start. It's actually one of the things my mama kicks ass at making. Considering it's one of the only things she's ever made me—forget Rice Krispie treats and grilled cheese and Jell-O and the stuff other kids' moms make for them—I guess it's a good thing she's good at it.

She moves around the kitchen easily, still knowing where everything is . . . just like she knew where the jewelry was. While she's pulling out the same mauve Tupperware jug Gran has used for this purpose as long as I can remember, I try to think of how to bring up the subject. But instead, she catches me off guard.

"You look happy, Holly. Is he making you happy?"

"Wha—what?"

"Happy. Is he making you happy?"

My mother being concerned about my happiness is so shocking that it knocks the truth from my lips before I can think to edit it. Or maybe it's the naive hope that she may actually care about the answer. Either way, I speak from the heart.

"I am. We had a bit of a rough start, but I think we've finally got our feet under us. Me walking out and coming here was probably the best thing I could've possibly done."

The Tupperware lid bounces off the counter and lands on the floor.

Mama looks at me, one hand cocked on her hip and the other raised to her lips. "You walked out on that man? Please tell me that isn't true."

My old defensiveness rises fast, and once again, I don't think before I speak.

"What would you have done if your husband's first wife cornered you at a benefit, telling you you were lucky number three and not the second wife like you'd thought, and sent you into a panic attack, making you realize you had to get out of that concrete jungle of a claustrophobic nightmare before you lost your friggin' mind?"

The hand at Mama's mouth also drops to her hips. "He's been married *three* times? But the news never says that. *Ever*. And he didn't tell you? Oh my, Holly. I don't like that he's keeping secrets. That's not the way a marriage is supposed to work. Trust me, as bad as I've been at them, I should know."

Her honest-to-God parental-sounding concern throws me off. And then I repeat her words in my head.

"Wait, what? How many times have you been married? I thought . . ."

Mama's gaze drops to the floor like it's the most fascinating thing she's ever seen, and I can't help but think the pink flush creeping up her cheeks is embarrassment. It's a new look on her.

When she looks at me a few moments later, it's to say, "Well, let's just say you're not the only one in the family to have a quickie Vegas wedding. Let's just hope you only have one."

That floor Mama found so goddamn interesting? My jaw is on it.

"You didn't think it was necessary to mention? I mean, seriously? How many?"

She mumbles something, and I'm out of my chair and closing in on her. "Mama, how many?"

"Two in Vegas, one in Reno, and one in Paducah."

"You've been married *four freaking times* and never once told your only daughter?"

Her posture crumples inward, making me regret my harsh words, even though I don't think I should. When Mama's shoulders shake and tears spill down her face, I'm even more stunned. I've *never* seen her cry. I didn't think she was physically capable of it.

"I know I've been a horrible mother, and I have no excuses. But your gran raised you better than I ever could have. I'm sorry for everything, Holly. I've made a mess of my life and yours *and* hers, and I'm trying to make amends. I'm just learning how."

I'm a sucker. I know it, but I've never seen this kind

of honesty from my mother before. Never had this kind of conversation with her before. Maybe this is our second chance?

There's really nothing else I can do but wrap my arms around her and let her tears soak into the cotton of my shirt.

Her words are muffled, but I can still make them out. "I didn't tell you about the weddings because I knew they weren't going to last. Nothing ever did. You already hated me, and I didn't want to give you any more reason to show you what a failure I was."

Of its own volition, my hand raises and smooths her big hair down her back. "Oh, Mama. I don't hate you."

"Yes, you do. You should. I killed my own mama. I'm a horrible person. I deserve to go straight to hell for what I've done, and instead your husband sends me on vacation."

Her body shakes harder with her sobs, and I can't even comprehend what's happening right now. But somehow, some way, the icy exterior I forged years ago around my heart to protect me from Mama's repeated disappointments and harsh words starts to melt.

After Mama and I pulled ourselves together and drank our sweet tea, she got glammed up and headed to B&B. She tried to talk me into coming with her, but I really wasn't in the mood to be on any kind of stage tonight, whether it's the karaoke one or just generally being on display in public.

Besides, I needed some time to adjust to what the hell happened this afternoon, and the emotions are running raw in me. So for the past hour I've been pouring them into lyric after lyric, feeling like this song is being ripped from my soul and somehow mending it together at the same time.

It's long since dark and closing in on seven when another knock comes at the door.

Who now? I seriously can't handle any more surprises. I wait a few moments, and when the knock doesn't come again, my tripped-up heart rate drops back to normal levels.

The roar of a diesel engine accelerating piques my curiosity, and I rise and cross to the door. Pushing the lace curtain aside a crack, I look out and see nothing. When I crane my head to one side, I catch the tail end of a brown truck driving away. *UPS.*

After unlocking the dead bolt, I pull the door open, and sure enough, a package the size of a shoebox is sitting on the purple porch.

I smile.

Crey. Is this what he was calling me about earlier?

I grab it and duck back inside before going for the kitchen knife and cutting it open. There's a note stuck to the bubble wrap. My heart rate kicks up for a whole different reason this time.

He's only been gone since yesterday, and I already miss him like crazy. I wish I was able to talk to him earlier, but my shock over Mama is pretty much off the charts.

I know I'm boots over brains in love with the man when just the sight of his handwriting makes me giddy.

Holly,
It's called The Executive, and you better damn sure be
screaming this executive's name when you come.
—Crey

What in the world?

I set the note aside and unwrap the package. It's a vibrator. A shiny silver vibrator. It's shaped strangely, but from what I know of vibrators, which admittedly isn't all that much, it's got the G-spot and clit action going on. My lady parts sit up and take notice just from my looking at it.

After the crazy-emotional afternoon and evening, a nice hot bath with a big glass or two of wine is just what I need to unwind . . . followed by a test drive of my new toy.

CHAPTER
SIXTEEN

Creighton

I'm in the middle of an episode of *Country Dreams* when my cell buzzes across my desk. I slap at it with my left hand, annoyed that someone is interrupting while I'm watching Holly belt out a song called "Independence Day," and unwilling to take my eyes off my laptop.

I grab the phone, fully intending to hit IGNORE, but when my eyes cut down to the screen, I see Holly's name. I hit PAUSE on my laptop, and answer immediately.

"Holly."

She breathes heavily into the phone for a beat before saying, "Hey."

"Are you okay?"

"Oh, I'm about to be a hell of a lot better than just okay. But your note said you wanted to hear me scream your name, Mr. Executive, so here I am, following orders."

Fuuuuck. My dick jumps in my pants. I totally forgot about the vibrator, completely and totally forgot about it. I'm not even sure how that's possible, but apparently it is.

All my concerns about today fall away at nothing more than the thought of her pleasure.

"Are you telling me that right now, you've got that vibrator buried in your sweet pussy?"

"And a plug up my ass."

"Jesus fucking Christ, Holly," I say on a groan. "You haven't made yourself come yet?"

"No. I wanted you to hear me."

"Good girl."

I pull the phone away from my ear, hit the button for speaker, and lay it on the desk. Then I reach for my belt and undo it, purposely letting the buckle clink together.

"Are you—?"

"I'm getting my cock out so I can jack myself off to the sound of you coming. I miss you, Holly. Miss your hot little cunt, your tight little ass, and those perfect fucking tits."

"Holy crap. I think I almost came just hearing you say that." Her voice shakes over the phone.

I smile. "Good."

As soon as I've got my hand wrapped around my cock, I realize I'm woefully unprepared, so I head to the bathroom, snag some lube, and make my way into the master suite, all the while telling Holly the dirty things I'd do to her if I were there.

"Because you liked having my cock in your ass, didn't

you?"

"I'm pretty sure I came until I almost blacked out, didn't I?"

"You're fucking perfect, woman," I say as I strip, settle myself on the bed, and lube up. "Now we're going to see how good you are at getting yourself off."

Her laugh makes my dick even harder. "I already know I'm good at that, Crey. *Trust me*. Lots of practice in the one-handed action department."

I groan at the visual and wrap my hand around my cock. "Okay, baby. You said you already have it inside you?"

"Yeah."

"How close are you to the edge?"

"Pretty freaking close."

"I want you to slow down, tease yourself for a minute."

"What do you think I've been doing?"

"Are you getting bossy with me, Holly?"

"Maybe. I really want to come." Her tone takes on just the whisper of a whine, her desperation bleeding into every word.

"Soon, baby, I promise. First I want you to circle your clit, bring yourself all the way to the edge."

Her moans and whimpers are driving me crazy, and I stroke myself right to the same goddamn edge.

"Crey, please. I need—"

"Turn up the vibe, baby, and then I want it nice and snug up inside that tight little pussy, pressing against your G-spot. I want you to take it deep like you'd take me. Get yourself there. All the way. I want to hear it right now. Because when I come all over my hand, I want to hear you screaming my name."

Her harsh *oh my God* precedes louder and louder moans. "Crey . . . I'm gonna. I have to . . . I can't . . ."

"Come for me, Holly. Right now. Right the fuck now."

My order is sharp because I'm teetering on the edge of control, my balls pulled up to the base of my cock, my orgasm about to blow.

"Crey!" Her moan approaches a scream and I wish, more than anything, I were there to see her face as pleasure drags her past the point of no return.

I lose my own ironclad control, and her name echoes in our bedroom. A few beats later, I drop my head back on the pillow.

Her voice comes through the phone. "Crey, are you still there?"

"I'm still here, baby. You just fucking destroyed me from over six hundred miles away."

A soft chuckle comes through the phone, followed by a few minutes of nothing but our heavy breathing as we both recover.

Eventually Holly speaks first. "I'm glad I caught you tonight. I'm sorry about earlier. Mama came home. She appreciated the vacation. So, thank you for that."

My hackles rise. "Your mother came home? Are you okay?" I grab the T-shirt I tossed aside and clean my mess off my hand and stomach. "Fuck, I should've stayed."

"It's okay, Crey. Don't freak out. It was actually . . . good. We talked. I think she and I might actually be in a semi-okay place at the moment. If you were still here,

I don't think that would've happened, so maybe things needed to happen like this."

The tension gripping me eases only a fraction. "Are you sure? Because, fuck, Holly, from what you've told me about your mother—"

"I know, but she's still my mama, for better or for worse, and if there's a chance it can be for the better, then I need to believe that maybe she has changed. I know I've set myself up for the fall before, but she actually seems different this time."

Bad feelings churn in my gut, but I can't bring myself to crush the hope in Holly's voice. All I can see is that little girl in the pictures at her gran's, wishing her mother would be like the other mothers and actually give a damn about her instead of the man-of-the-minute in her life.

I choose my words carefully. "I support you, Holly. So whatever you decide is best for you, I'm going to support that too."

The soft laugh that echoes through the phone slips into my chest and grips my heart.

"You're right, Crey. This is as real as it gets. I love you. I'll talk to you in the morning?"

"Absolutely. I love you too. Good night, baby."

When I hang up, I'm smiling. I need to figure this shit out with my uncle tomorrow, because I'm flying south ASAP.

CHAPTER
SEVENTEEN

Holly

Head aching a little from the wine, but thankfully not hung over, I roll out of bed and tiptoe down the stairs. Gran's bedroom door is wide open, and it appears that Mama never came home last night.

I shove down the sarcastic voice inside me that wants to say, *Shocking, really*? Like I told Creighton, I need to believe she's changed.

I brew a cup of coffee and peek out the window to the front porch. I'm still grateful people have decided I'm not really worth noticing, even in this small town. Grabbing one of Gran's hand-knitted afghans, I go out onto the front porch and curl up in the rocking chair.

It's dawn, still cold enough out that steam is rising off the pond across the road. There's a peacefulness here that doesn't exist anywhere else.

Crey's right; I'm not ready to sell this house. I may not make it back here as often as I'd like, but having this place as my haven seems imperative. Coming back to my roots was the right choice. No matter how many fans may know my name, and no matter how crazy life may get, I'm just a simple girl from Gold Haven, Kentucky.

And now, after coming home and seeing this place through my slightly jaded eyes—and through Creighton's eyes—I'm okay with being that girl. Just like everyone else, I'm the sum total of my experiences, and I wouldn't be where I am today, married to the man I'm crazy in love with, if I didn't walk the path that was set out in front of me.

As I rock in the chair on Gran's porch and watch the sunrise paint the sky, I can't help but be grateful for the opportunities I've been given. Memories of hardships fade away, overshadowed by all the goodness.

A while later my cell phone rings from inside the house, interrupting my solitude and general contentment with the world. Levering myself off the chair, I cross the porch and push open the door to grab it off the counter and answer it.

Obviously, I'm hoping it's Crey. But it's not—it's Tana.

"Hey, girl, what's going on?" I haven't talked to her since I told her why I left New York the second time just before I headed to Gold Haven.

"Have you seen the papers or the gossip sites today?"

My stomach drops to my feet. "I'm not going to like what you have to say, am I?"

"Oh shit. You haven't."

"Nope. No tabloids on my front porch here." I swallow back the rising apprehension and drop into a chair. "How bad is it?"

"It's pretty bad, babe. Your mama sold a tell-all exclusive to *Yapper* that they posted about ten minutes ago. And this morning, the news also broke about your husband being sued by his own shareholders for corporate fraud or something like that. That was in the *Wall Street Journal*, not *Yapper*, but I didn't know about it until I read the *Yapper* article and they linked to it. Your names are on everyone's lips today."

"What?"

I'm glad I'm not holding my coffee cup any longer. It would be shattered on the floor right now.

"You know how they say no publicity is bad publicity? Well, today let's really hope that's true for your sake."

I shove out of the chair and stride to Gran's bedroom, and sure enough, all of Mama's stuff is gone. Stumbling back against the warped oak door, I slide down it and drop my head between my knees. My hand shakes so much, I can barely hold the phone to my ear.

"What did she say?" I whisper.

Disappointment, disgust, and anger well up inside me, my stomach twisting and flopping. I gave her the benefit of the doubt like the sucker I am. What was I thinking?

Tana sounds almost hesitant as she speaks. "I think Creighton probably got the worst of it. I had no idea he was married in college. The whole thing was buried. Rumor has it the girl faked a pregnancy to snag him, and then when she realized he wasn't getting a dime from his uncle, pretended to lose the baby. Everything about you just mostly makes you sound like a girl crazy in love with her husband."

The sick feeling multiplies as my neck and cheeks grow hot. I'm responsible for Creighton's personal business being spread all over the pages of a rag—personal business I knew nothing about.

Annika was pregnant? Or at least pretended to be? He left that out, along with the fact that he was going to get sued. Did he know that was coming? I remember the tense set of his shoulders when he answered the call from Cannon. He must have known. But why didn't he share that with me?

"Tell me about Creighton getting sued."

"You really didn't know?"

Tana's question comes out as shocked, and a small sliver of me can't help but wonder what else Crey may not be telling me. I hate that kernel of doubt.

I bolt up off the floor, and begin pacing the room. "Please, Tana? I wouldn't be asking you if I knew."

"Shit. And here I thought you were just the fucking queen of keeping secrets."

"What are you talking about?"

My crazy feelings crash into each other like cars at a malfunctioning stoplight. Frustration wins out, and I want to reach through the phone and shake it out of her.

"He bought Homegrown fucking Records, Holly. For you."

Blood rushes through my ears, deafening me.

"What?" I whisper.

"Holy fuck, you really didn't know?"

"No, I didn't know." My voice is getting louder as the shock turns to confusion and disbelief.

"Shit," she whispers. "That's kinda huge. How could he not tell you?"

I drop my head back against the wall.

"What else hasn't he told me?" I mumble.

"I don't know, babe. He's your husband."

"So, what do I do now?" I don't know if I'm asking myself, Tana, or the universe in general. Luckily for me, Tana has an answer.

"Get your ass back to Nashville. Come to my place and lay low."

My phone beeps with another incoming call. I pull it away from my face, once again expecting to see Creighton's name on the screen. But it's not. It's Chance.

"Shit. Chance is calling me too. I better take it."

"He's gonna tell you the same thing that I am. Get your ass back to town, and your people will circle the wagons."

"Thank you for the heads-up. Now to do damage control on my life."

"You got this, babe. Love you."

I hit the button to flip over to Chance's call.

"You heard the news that you're news?" he says without preamble.

"Yep. Just now."

"Good. Get yourself back to town. You're gonna lay low and finish your songs. Boone says he'll put you up so you're out of the public eye. I'll send you Garcia to get the songs finalized, and then you and the band can practice at Boone's. We're going to cut that album as fast as we fucking can."

It's so much information to take in, I'm reeling. "Slow down, Chance. This is all—"

"No time to slow down, kid. As of this morning, you're the girl everyone's talking about. We need to ride the wave before it goes south."

I should appreciate his opportunistic business sense, but I need a second to breathe. "It's my goddamn life, Chance. Not a fucking wave."

"I know, doll. But all you can do is hold on and enjoy the ride. Call me when you get to Boone's."

I pause in my pacing, the phone still to my ear, and I listen to nothing but dead air for ten seconds before I snap out of it enough to hang up.

Seriously? That's it? He didn't even stop and ask me if I *wanted* to stay at Boone's. I planned to crash behind Tana's gates. I grit my teeth, knowing I'm about to ride into the shitstorm of the century.

My stomach twists and turns with guilt. Mama better be long gone, because if I track her down, there's no telling what I'll say or do. And Creighton . . . I don't even know what to think. The guilt that I'm the reason his past is smeared across the tabloids fights with the hurt that he didn't tell me he bought the label and is facing serious legal issues because of it.

This is supposed to be as real as it gets, and yet he said nothing. Why? And why hasn't he called me today? I stare down at my phone and quickly search for his contact. I tap his cell number, trying to figure out what I'm going to say.

But no need—the call goes straight to voice mail.

I call again.

And again.

And again.

Nothing.

Finally, I call his office. Instead of the receptionist I got the last time, I get a prerecorded message thanking me for my call before offering me the number of the PR department at Karas International. I blink as I lower my phone to the counter.

Seriously, Creighton? What is this?

The only thing I can fathom is that they've been overrun with calls about today's news. For a moment I think about calling the PR department and asking them to have the boss call his *wife*. But I decide that's not the best course of action.

My imagination is jumping all over the place. Is he locked inside some kind of super-top-secret meeting that he can't get away from? Was the Homegrown deal the reason he stood me up when I needed to be back in Nashville? So many secrets, and I'm not privy to a single goddamn one of them.

So much for this being as real as it gets. Because real is telling your spouse that you've bought their record label. Real is telling your spouse that the shit is about to hit the fan because you bought their record label.

And from my side of the fence, real is apologizing that I opened my goddamn mouth to my mama and gave her anything to tell the press.

I want to rage at him and apologize all at the same time.

Why is love so damned complicated?

When he still hasn't called by the time I'm shoving my bags in the Cadillac, rage is winning out. *Where the hell is my husband?*

The bowling bag is the last thing I put in the backseat. I thought about leaving it, but said *screw it*. I have a feeling that *screw it* is going to be my mantra of the day.

Your mama sells you out to a tabloid? *Screw it.*

Your husband buys your record label and doesn't mention it? *Screw it.*

Your husband gets sued after buying said record label and doesn't mention that either? *Screw it.*

I slam the car into gear and tear out of the drive. I've got one stop to make before I leave town, so I crank the wheel in the direction of Logan's service station.

I'm pretty sure the tires on the Caddy are smoking when I squeal to a halt. *Screw it.*

I fling the door open and hip check it shut. *Screw it.*

I march across the pavement and throw open the door, not slowing to ring the bell for service. The music is once again blaring, so I stalk to the stereo and slap a hand on the power button. *Screw it.*

Logan's head jerks up from the Mustang. "Again? What the hell is your problem with Zeppelin?"

"They were all men. That's enough." Although I'm not too happy with womankind—or motherkind—today either.

Logan leans back against the cherry-red front end of

the car and crosses his arms over his chest.

"Karas again?"

I throw my hands up in the air. "Obviously! Well, him and my mama."

I pace the garage, stepping over air hoses and metal legs of the huge car lifts as I spill the entire sordid story.

Logan's eyes are wide when I finish. "You've had a rough morning, girl."

"No kidding."

"What can I do?"

I recall the reasons I came here to begin with. "Two things, if you wouldn't mind."

"Anything you need. All you have to do is ask."

I briefly consider asking him to track down my mother, but decide that's the worst possible idea.

"Can you sell my Pontiac?"

"Of course. Just tell me where to send the money."

"I'll worry about that later." I pause in my pacing and face him. "I also need you to get a locksmith out to my gran's and have the locks changed for me. If you get word my mama's back in town, I want her arrested again for breaking and entering if she tries to get back inside. The house is mine, and I don't want her in it. Last time she stole stuff, and I'm finished with that crap."

"Consider it done."

My temper cooling slightly, I cross over to him, lean up on my tiptoes, and press a kiss to his cheek. "You're a good man, Logan Brantley. A really good man."

His cheeks flush red, but he smiles. "And don't you forget it, Holly Wickman. You call me if you ever need anything."

He turns and grabs a slip of paper off the workbench and scribbles his number down with a fat pencil. "Nashville ain't too far, and if you need me, I'll be there. Just say the word."

I'm not sure how to take that, so I just say, "Thank you. I'm glad my car died at this particular gas station."

"Me too, honey. Me too."

I'm at a crossroads in my life, both literally and figuratively. I can head southwest toward Nashville and hide behind Boone or Tana's gates. Or I can head northeast, into the shitstorm surrounding my husband. A shitstorm that I helped make worse on a personal level because of what I shared with Mama.

I think about what Creighton said to me just before we hung up last night.

"I support you, Holly. So whatever you decide is best for you, I'm going to support that too."

As pissed as I am that he didn't tell me about Homegrown, I owe him the same thing—my support. I ran from him twice before, but this time I'm running straight to him. I'm not saying I won't ask him what the hell he was thinking by not telling me, but this isn't a game.

It's the fight of my life.

CHAPTER
EIGHTEEN

Creighton

Holly isn't answering my calls, and I'm about to lose my shit. If she runs again, I have a feeling I might not be able to find her so easily this time. I've been trying to reach her for hours, and if I don't get a response in the next twenty minutes, I'm going to start tracking her credit cards.

We were already in lockdown when the article in the *Wall Street Journal* went live. Some poor red-faced associate came in holding a printout of the article and the piece in *Yammer*. It's safe to say that I shouldn't be meeting Holly's mother anytime soon, for both our sakes.

I'm pacing the conference room, calling Holly again, when the door is shoved open.

"Honey, you called?"

I drop the phone from my ear when Holly struts in, suitcase in tow. Every head in the room swivels toward her.

"Don't you know how to answer your phone, woman?"

"Oh no, he didn't."

The words are whispered, and I think they come from an associate at the end of the long table. Rather than annoying me, his words remind me that my office is not the place for this discussion.

Stalking across the room, I stop in front of my wife. She should be spitting mad, but she's smiling. That's almost more disconcerting.

"Hey, baby. I missed you," she says.

"Everyone out," I order, and the room clears within sixty seconds, partners and associates alike shuffling by us without making eye contact.

"What are you doing here?" I ask, wondering if Holly is going to drop the act and go for the jugular the moment we're alone. But instead, she says something completely unexpected.

"I support you, Crey. Whatever decisions you made about what to tell me or not tell me, I'm assuming you made them for a reason."

"Holly—"

"I'm not done."

My lips quirk up into a smile. "Then by all means, please continue."

She straightens her posture, and I'm not sure if that's a good sign or not. "Don't get me wrong, I'm disappointed that you didn't tell me about Homegrown, but I'm assuming you had a reason for not telling me. So instead of running to Nashville like I was told, I decided it was time to show you that I know how to run to you just as well as I know how to run away. So here I am. This shitstorm wouldn't exist if you'd never met me, and my place is right beside you while we wade through the muck."

Hearing her say those words unleashes something fiercely proud and protective within me. "You're a hell of a woman, Holly Karas."

"Because of you, I'm starting to believe that."

I lift both hands and frame her face. "Fuck, am I glad to see you. And for the record, if you'd run back to Nashville, I would've come after you again. Every time. Until you tell me to stop. And probably even after that."

Threading my fingers through her hair, I lower my lips to hers.

"Like I'd ever tell you to stop," she whispers before I take her mouth with mine.

When Holly leans up on her toes, hands gripping my shoulders, I pull my lips away and untangle my hands from her hair.

"Might as well just climb me."

I drop my hands and cup her ass, lifting her and carrying her to the conference table. Lowering her onto a section not covered in papers, I lay her back and skim my lips up her neck, my teeth scraping along the tendons. Her moans break the silence of the conference room, and all I want to do is fuck her until neither of us can walk.

The conference room door swings open.

"Seriously, Crey? We don't have time for this right now."

Cannon doesn't even bother to clear his throat to give us a polite warning or look away when we break apart.

"Get the fuck out," I growl.

"You pay me too much money to let you fuck around when we need to be fixing shit."

Holly wiggles out from underneath me, and my body is not happy to have her go.

"Cannon, I don't believe we've formally met in person."

She rounds the table and holds out her hand, not showing the slightest concern that he walked in on us. My wife has nerves of steel, and I find that sexy as hell—just like I find everything about her.

Cannon shakes her hand, a small smile on his face. "Nice to meet you, Holly."

"I'd say likewise, but I don't really like you. Actually, I kind of think you're a jerk. And now I know for sure you're a total cock-blocker."

Having never been faced with a woman like Holly before, Cannon stiffens and his eyes cut to me. The look on his face says, *Do something, man.*

I raise my eyebrows in response, clearly communicating, *Not a fucking chance.*

"Well," Cannon says, dropping Holly's hand and clearing his throat, "we really need to continue our strategy session so we can get this issue handled. We've got less than twenty-four hours before you've got to stand up in front of a room full of investors, and we need a solid explanation."

"There's nothing more to strategize at this point. The investors aren't stupid. They deserve more than a *solid explanation*. They deserve the truth, and that's exactly what I'm going to give them."

"Fuck, Crey. The truth? That you lost your fucking mind over a piece of ass, so you married her and bought her goddamn record label because you didn't like that they were bullying her around?"

Holly's harshly drawn breath pierces the momentary silence before I surge across the room. My fist flies before I even consider what I'm doing. My knuckles crack against Cannon's jaw, sending pain rocketing from my hand up my arm, but I don't fucking care because all I want is for him to shut his goddamn mouth.

Cannon stumbles back, reaching out to the paneled wall to keep from falling on his ass. "What the hell, man?"

"You're fired. And you're fucking lucky I don't kill you."

"Creighton, wait." Holly's voice is quiet, but firm. "He's clearly an idiot, but he's your best friend."

"Which is why he's not dead."

"Crey—"

"Shut your fucking mouth, Cannon."

"No, Cannon, open it and apologize. And then maybe my husband will give you your job back."

"No fucking way," I say, my tone deadly serious. The man is lucky he's still breathing. No one talks about Holly like that.

But my former best friend ignores me and shoves off the wall. Wiping the back of his hand across his face, he looks to Holly.

"I'm sorry, Holly. I apologize for running my mouth like a jackass." When he looks at me, he says, "I'm just looking out for you, Crey. I swear, I just didn't think. And that's how the press is going to see it too. We just need to be prepared."

I open my mouth to tell him to go fuck himself again, but Holly comes toward me and lays a hand on my arm.

"You can't fire him over this, Crey. Hit him again, maybe. But then go take him out for a beer and get back to solid ground. He's just looking out for you, and he's been important to you for a lot longer than I have. I won't be the reason that breaks. So, figure your shit out."

Then she looks to Cannon. "But if you ever call me a piece of ass again, I'll immortalize you in a song, and I promise, you will not like how it ends. And that'll be after I take my best shot at knocking your perfect freaking teeth out."

Turning back to me, she adds, "I'm going to go back to the penthouse now to try to finish up these songs and do damage control with Chance. I'll be waiting when you've finished up your meetings. I actually feel like blowing off my diet and cooking tonight. So make sure you bring your appetite."

She leans up on her tiptoes once more, and I decide that it's one of my favorite moves. Her lips press lightly against mine. My hand curves around her hip, anchoring her to me.

When she lowers back down to her heels, I release my hold on her. "I'm glad you're here, Holly. Really fucking glad."

"Nowhere else I'd rather be."

Her lips curl into a smile, but it's still not quite as wide as the one I saw on her face on *Country Dreams*. Once this is all over, I'll make sure she has even more to smile about.

"Is your kitchen stocked?"

I nod. "Yes, but I'll have a car take you home."

She doesn't argue. "Okay, Crey. I'll make something that'll keep, no matter how late you get home."

Warm contentment settles in my chest. This is an entirely new feeling for me. Working as a team, supporting each other.

"I'll be home as soon as I can, baby."

Her smile as she leaves the room only ratchets up that contented feeling, lacing it with determination to put this behind us as quickly as I can so we can move forward.

When the door shuts behind her, Cannon grips his jaw with his hand and cracks it. "One more meeting with the lawyers. You lay out whatever plan you've got. They'll tell you it's inadvisable. You'll decide, fuck it, I'm CEO and therefore I can do whatever the fuck I want, and you'll do it anyway." He stills his movements and pins me with the blue eyes I've known since boarding school. "Is that about how this is going to go?"

I grin. "Yes."

"Then let's get it over with quickly so you can get home to the wife."

I hold out my hand, and he shakes it. "Sounds good."

CHAPTER
NINETEEN

Holly

I'm going all out tonight. Fried chicken, cornbread, baked beans, steamed broccoli, and cherry cobbler. I know, the broccoli is the odd man out, but it's my nod at attempting to stick to my nutrition plan.

I've got Elle King cranked up, and I'm bobbing along to "America's Sweetheart" when I feel him behind me. I have no explanation for it. Crey just has a presence, and apparently it's one that my body is absolutely and completely attuned to.

"Hey, baby. Hope you're hungry." I lift the chicken out of the boiling oil and set it aside to drain before I turn to face him.

"Goddamn, I don't know what smells better—you or the chicken."

I snort. "I'm going to assume that's a compliment and just roll with it."

He leans down to press a kiss to my lips. "It is. And I'll be having you for dessert."

I haven't had an orgasm since the one that I had during our phone sex last night. And damn—has it really only been one night? My body is wound so tight that you couldn't prove it by me.

"That sounds fabulous."

Crey turns and sets his briefcase on the bar stool, and I can't help but smile at the fact that he didn't set it down before he came to me. He removes his coat, lays it over the briefcase, and comes to stand beside me at the stove.

"What are you feeding me, woman?"

"Are you in caveman mode now? See woman, she cook. She must feed man," I say in my best caveman voice.

"If you want to play that game later, I'll drag you back to my cave."

I shake my head, a laugh spilling from my lips. Even in the midst of this shitstorm, we're laughing and joking. That means something, right? How you limp along during the bad times means so much more than how you glide along during the good ones, right?

"You're crazy, Crey. And I love that about you."

He leans down and this time, sweeps my hair aside and brushes kisses along my neck. I try to swallow back the moan, but it escapes anyway. Even so, reality intrudes.

"Baby, I've got hot oil on the stove. You need to let me finish frying the chicken, and then we can pick this up."

He growls—*growls*—before backing away. "You al-

149

ready open a bottle of wine?"

"Nope. Left that to you. I'd probably pick something that clashed horribly with the masterpiece we're about to eat."

"You realize I don't give a shit if you picked the wrong wine, don't you?"

"I know, but still. I didn't want to start drinking without you. Your wine is the good stuff, so I probably would've had one glass, and it would've been so delicious that I would've needed another glass. And maybe another. Especially after this disaster of a day. And then you would've come home to burned-to-crap fried chicken, hard-as-a-brick cornbread, sloppy baked beans, squishy broccoli, and flambéed cherry cobbler."

Crey pauses in his reach into the wine fridge. "You made all that?"

"Uh-huh. And it's going to be fabulous."

"Well, damn. I don't even know what to say to that."

"You don't have to say anything. Just eat it. And then me. After."

I snap my mouth shut. *I can't believe I just said that. Wait—yes, I can.*

Crey lifts the bottle of wine from its rack and closes the door. "Oh, baby, you feeling neglected? Because I'll eat that sweet pussy of yours for days."

A shiver of awareness shoots through me. "Days aren't really necessary. I'd settle for a really vigorous hour."

Crey's grin should qualify him as the sexiest man alive. Those sharp cheekbones, dark eyes, and his square jaw, every feature is beautifully accentuated by his smile.

"Damn. You are one sexy son of a bitch. You know that, right?"

If possible, his grin widens. "Well, if I didn't, I do now."

"I'm suddenly not very hungry."

The grin morphs into a lazy smile. "Patience, baby. Patience. Besides, a man only gets to eat like this once in a while, and I'm not missing out on my shot. But I think dessert can wait until after."

"Deal. Let's eat. Fast."

There are so many things we need to talk about, but I decide they can wait until morning. Tonight, I just want to revel in the good, and pretend none of the bad exists. It'll all be waiting for us in the morning.

But tonight . . . tonight we only get once. I'm not going to waste it.

CHAPTER
TWENTY

Creighton

At noon the following day, I stand on a podium, the Karas International Inc. logo emblazoned on nearly every surface in the huge auditorium. The room is filled to capacity; it's standing room only. There's nothing like gossip to bring every interested body out in droves.

But today, they're not going to get gossip. Today, they're going to get the truth.

"Welcome to Karas International's Annual Investor Day. As chairman of the board and chief executive officer, it's my pleasure to welcome you. I'd like to open with a statement that will address what I'm sure is a matter many of you have come seeking answers about—the purchase of Homegrown Records by an independent entity owned by me personally, which prompted a lawsuit filed by a shareholder on behalf of Karas International. The suit alleges that as a company executive and member of its board, this purchase breaches my duty of loyalty both to the company and to you, its shareholders."

A few whispers start in the audience, and I can tell it's because no one expected me to confront this issue head-on. Which amuses me, because I'm Creighton fucking Karas. Head-on is what I do.

"I'd like to be the first to tell you that the allegations contained in that suit are complete and utter bullshit. The purchase of Homegrown was not in any way made to usurp an opportunity that would have been appropriate to our company's current or contemplated business port-folio, nor would it have been beneficial to Karas International. For the record, Homegrown has already cost me over thirty million dollars of capital infusion just to keep the damn thing running."

The whispers in the audience begin to grow in vol-ume, which annoys me. "If you'll hold your comments until the end, I'll take your questions until you don't have any more. But I'd appreciate your courtesy so I can finish my statement."

A hush instantly falls over the room, and I continue.

"However, I will agree that the proper procedure to avoid any hint of impropriety and to forestall any grounds for the allegations supporting the suit would have been to have the independent members of the board of direc-tors vote on the transaction. I'm sure you're wondering why I didn't go that route, and I only have one answer for you. Have you ever been so absolutely in love that you've stopped thinking about practicalities entirely?"

A titter rolls through the room, and I pause for a moment to let them absorb my comment before I continue.

"I'm a man in love with an amazing woman, and while that argument will not hold weight in a court of law, in a court of public opinion, I think it makes perfect sense. The purchase of Homegrown was meant to be a surprise belated wedding present for my new wife, so I acted quickly, and perhaps without thinking things through in my normal logical fashion, because I wanted to do it before my beautiful, intelligent bride realized what I was doing."

I'm pretty sure every female in the crowd is now sighing. Glancing up from the podium, I see Holly standing in the back corner, and she's lifting a hand to her face and dabbing at the underside of her eye.

I don't try to hold the smile back. "So, there you go. That's the explanation I have for you. Now I'll take your questions."

The flurry starts, but a booming voice cuts through the din. "You really think that ridiculous explanation is going to matter? Not likely, Creighton. I thought you were smarter than that."

With that, my uncle Damon turns on his heel and leaves the room.

I spend over an hour answering investor questions before my portion of the presentation is over. Holly is waiting at the back of the auditorium, and I stride to where she stands and pull her into my arms.

"You know how to give one hell of a speech, Crey," she says, speaking in muffled words into my chest.

"I meant every word of it."

"Is Homegrown really my wedding present?"

I loosen my grip and step back a fraction so I can look down into her eyes. "Yes. It was always for you."

Her brow furrows, concern shading her eyes. "Does that mean you expect me to run it?"

"If you want to; you can do whatever you want. The management team I've got in place now is starting to turn things around, but if you want to get involved with the business side of things, you're more than welcome."

I pause to tuck a lock of hair behind her ear. "I think that'd be sexy as fuck, if you want to know the truth . . . my wife, the CEO, running her own empire."

I groan as my dick jerks against my zipper. *Not the time or the place, buddy.* A small smile spreads over Holly's face, which doesn't help matters.

"Crey."

The sound of Cannon's voice, however, deflates my hard-on. Holly called it when she referred to him as a cock-blocker. Releasing Holly with one arm, I turn.

"What do you need?"

"What are you going to do about Damon?"

"Besides take a hit out on him?"

Cannon's eyes widen only slightly. "I know a guy."

"Jesus. Fuck, Cannon. I'm joking."

He shrugs. "Desperate times."

"And that's called conspiracy, and I don't care to find

out the New York prison system's policy on conjugal visits."

At this, Holly snorts. "Can I second that?"

A tall, thin black man approaches us. He's the associate from the conference room who made the "Oh no, he didn't" comment when Holly walked in.

"Mr. Karas, Mr. Cramer wanted to run one more idea by you, given your uncle's latest outburst. Could we have a few minutes of your time in the conference room across the hall?"

I look to Holly, and she says, "Crey, do your thing. I'll be waiting. I'm feeling an epic song about revenge coming on, à la Carrie Underwood's 'Two Black Cadillacs' or maybe 'Good-bye, Earl.'"

Leaning down, I brush a kiss across her cheek. "I love you, woman. I'll be right back."

"Give 'em hell. And I love you too."

I follow Cannon and the associate—I really need to get his name—to the conference room across the hall from the auditorium.

My lawyer, Cramer is waiting, and he looks less than amused. I suppose it's lucky that he works for me and not the other way around.

"Save your breath, Cramer. You didn't approve before, and you don't approve now. I also know you're not going to approve of what I'm going to do next."

"And what's that, Mr. Karas?" he asks, the skepticism in his tone thinly veiled.

One of the largest negative aspects of this suit is the element of fear that has slipped away from my persona.

This will be remedied. I'm Creighton fucking Karas, and the world will not question my judgment again when this is over.

"My uncle may be brave enough to take me on in front of a crowd, but we'll see how he feels about taking me on man-to-man."

The lawyer's silver eyebrows hit his equally silver hairline. "That's highly inadvisable."

"Consider it a family matter and none of your concern." My words carry the unmistakable weight of authority.

He swallows. "Mr. Karas, we have your best interests in mind here. I'm sure you understand."

"Of course, Mr. Cramer, but sometimes the only thing a bully understands is a bigger bully. It's time the gloves come off. I'm done with his bullshit."

"You're not going to listen to a logical, reasoned argument, no matter what I say, are you?"

"There's no reasoning with my uncle, so no. Save your breath."

"Fine." Cramer nods. "We'll leave you to it. Please call us if we can be of further assistance."

I turn and head for the door. "Cannon, walk out with me?"

He's on my heels as we hit the threshold.

"You're not staying for the rest of Investor Day?" he asks. "You have a closing keynote."

I give him a sideways glance. "You think I don't know that? I'll try to be back in time. If I'm not, extend the dog-and-pony show. You've got promo videos and PowerPoints up the ass. Use something."

"And if that doesn't work?"

I stop, and my eyes cut to Holly. She's curled up in a chair, scribbling in the journal resting on her knee. She's so fucking beautiful, and I'd walk through a thousand shit-storms like the one swirling around us just to watch her like this.

Not looking at Cannon, I say, "Improvise. That's why I pay you the big bucks." I take a step toward Holly, but pause when he lays a hand on my arm.

"Crey."

I glance back at him. "What?"

"Damon is fucking crazy. What he's doing—his issue with you—that's not based in logic. It never has been. Be careful. I don't trust him, and I don't think you should either."

I inhale, long and slow. "I know. This has been a long time coming."

"Good luck, man."

Cannon peels off and heads back in the direction of the auditorium, and I cross the half dozen yards between Holly and me. She's so involved in her writing that she doesn't notice me until I crouch in front of her.

"I bet if I were naked, you'd notice me quicker."

Her head jerks up, and her smile is quick and bright.

"Damn straight, I would. That dick of yours demands attention."

"Later. Definitely."

"Count on it. After all, I hear I got a hell of a wedding present, which means you've got a hell of a thank-you coming."

"Maybe I should book the room at the Plaza?"

"Screw the Plaza. Let's go back to Vegas. I didn't get nearly enough time to enjoy that villa at Caesar's."

I smile, thankful she's not losing her mind over the Homegrown acquisition. "Deal. We sort this out, and you and I are going to high roll it in Vegas."

Holly leans forward and threads her fingers through my hair. "I'm going to head back to the penthouse to finish this song and pack. So, hurry up and sort it out."

"I'll consider those my marching orders."

Her lips press against mine, and while I want to seize control, I'm aware of the people moving around us, their eyes on us. I pull away.

"I'll call you as soon as I'm on my way."

"You better."

Another quick kiss and then I step away.

I don't realize that the next time I see her, everything I think I know about myself will have changed irrevocably.

CHAPTER
TWENTY-ONE

Creighton

I go first to my aunt and uncle's penthouse in the city, but I'm informed by the doorman, who has been a fixture in the building for as long as I can remember, that my uncle's already been and gone back to Westchester. Thanking him for the information, I slide back into the backseat of the Bentley.

"Looks like we're headed to the estate, Michael," I tell my driver.

"Very good, sir. I'm assuming we're in a hurry?"

"Aren't we always?"

I catch his grin in the rearview mirror. "Of course."

Midday traffic is thankfully lighter than normal, and I cruise through the e-mails piled up in my in-box before I read through the top stories reporting on my impassioned opening remarks at Investor Day.

CREIGHTON KARAS: EXECUTIVE IN LOVE.
THIS TIME IT'S FOR REAL, LADIES.
This morning at Karas International's annual Investor Day, Creighton Karas publicly announced that his acquisition of Homegrown Records was an impulsive move fueled by his feelings for his new bride. He claims that allegations of self-dealing and breach of fiduciary duty leveled in a shareholder derivative suit filed by the executive's own uncle are baseless given the company's portfolio of holdings. Further, Karas claims that a purchase of Homegrown by Karas International would have been detrimental to the health of the company and the best interest of its shareholders, given Homegrown's precarious financial situation. Homegrown, which has been hemorrhaging money since . . .

I skim the rest of the article and several others like it, but it seems that the court of public opinion is indeed turning in my favor.

Now, if I can get my uncle to take my offer and sell his shares in Karas International, then this problem will be solved and I can move on to taking Holly back to Vegas, and if I have my way, on a real honeymoon. I think she'd enjoy Europe after she gets her next record cut.

The beauty of my solution of having my uncle sell his shares is simple—he can't maintain his shareholder deriv-ative suit if he's no longer a shareholder. Clean and elegant. Even my lawyers would be proud.

By the time we pull up to the tall, ornate iron gates

of the sprawling Westchester estate that was arguably my childhood home, I have my entire speech planned. The gate slides open immediately, and Michael drives through. A blanket of crisp white snow blankets what I know is a manicured lawn with perfect shrubbery. It has never been graced by a swing set. Tag has never been played here. The ornamental trees have never been climbed.

Instead, Greer actually had tea parties, archery lessons, cotillion training, and etiquette instruction. Nine days out of ten, I was banished to my room when I was home, but sneaked out and stole books from the library on economics, finance, philosophy, and anything else that I thought could help me learn enough to make more money than my uncle.

I studied him. Mimicked his moves in the foreign exchange markets. Cashed in and got out to invest in business with people and assets instead of numbers and paper. I took my company public and made billions. And then he came and bought chunks of *my* stock, and his ownership of a piece of my company was eating away at the rest of it like a cancer. It's time for him to be excised.

I won't stand for it any longer. I built my empire with my own sweat, guts, and determination, and I defend what's mine. My uncle has forgotten that I am just as ruthless as he is. I learned from his example, after all. His reminder will be fierce and swift.

Michael slows to a stop in the circular drive of the ten-thousand-square-foot Georgian-style mansion.

"I won't be long," I say, reaching for the door handle and pushing it open.

"Yes, sir."

I make my way to the front door, and it swings open wide before I reach it.

"Elisabetta, it's good to see you again."

The housekeeper, who has served my aunt and uncle in near silence for as long as I can remember, nods. "This way, Mr. Creighton."

She leads me to my uncle's study and shuts the door behind me with a quiet click.

Damon is seated in an oversized antique leather chair that looks like it held a Russian tsar. Knowing Damon, it probably did. The Louis XIV desk is the size of a pool table, and the top is spotless, but for a sleek laptop on a leather blotter and a single Mont Blanc pen.

"Figured you'd show up. It's always good to be proven right." His eyes are narrowed on me, and his tone clearly says he's not pleased with my presence.

"Damon."

"Creighton."

"I don't expect you to offer me a seat. I always enjoy being proven right as well."

His mouth twists into a mockery of a smile. "I don't know what you think coming here is going to accomplish, but you might as well say what you've got to say and get out. Know in advance that you're wasting my time."

I imagine that my own smile is just as sardonic as his. I step closer and lower myself into one of his chairs for the sole purpose of knowing that it pisses him off. I enjoy towering over him, but I enjoy pissing him off more. His scowl gratifies every part of me.

"I came to end this, because quite frankly, Damon, you're wasting my time, and I'm fucking sick of it. I've got better things to do than dicking around with all this petty activist shareholder bullshit, and so do you. We both know it. You've hated me since I was a kid; I don't particularly care why. But we're both adults, and we're both businessmen. So how about we talk in terms that we both understand and respect—money. I want your shares. What's it going to take to get you out of my company and out of my fucking life?"

Damon's eyes, dark like my own, harden even more, but there's something else there that I can't identify. I'm reminded of Cannon's comment because in this moment, my uncle looks more than his normal shrewd and cutting self.

"You want my shares? You can have them." He sits forward, pressing his palms on the desk, and stands halfway out of his chair. "All you have to do is change your fucking last name and take it off your goddamn company."

What the fuck?

His request rings in my head, and my brain spins to find a motive or logic behind his words. He's fucking crazy.

"What the hell are you talking about, old man?" My words come out low and harsh.

Damon pushes away from the desk and stands tall. He's six foot one, which means I still top him by two inches. Feeling the need to establish dominance once again, I rise as well.

His face has morphed into the most twisted expression of perverted pleasure I've ever beheld as he tilts his head and studies me.

"You don't deserve that name. You never fucking did. Your whore of a mother got it for you by seducing my little brother. She ruined his fucking life. Killed him."

I suck in a breath but my lungs are burning, as if all the oxygen in this room couldn't satisfy them. *What is he saying?*

"Explain yourself before I fucking beat it out of you."

The evil light of perverse pleasure burns in his eyes. "You've never wondered why Greer actually looks Greek and you don't? Oh, you've got Mediterranean heritage, but it didn't come from this family."

Everything inside me goes cold. I become intrinsically aware of every unconscious function of my body. Every *tha-thunk* of my heart. The *whoosh* of blood through my ears. Each blink of my eyes. Every shallow, indrawn breath and shaky exhalation. The sensation of my stomach on the floor at my feet.

"What the fuck are you saying?" I roar.

Visions of my father—my swarthy, very Greek father—filter through my brain. My mother was a brunette as well. I always assumed I took after her more than him, but my looks never raised suspicion.

"Don't you get it, Crey? The only reason you weren't born a fucking bastard is because your mother seduced my brother into marrying her before you were born. She got knocked up by a married man, and her family threw her out. My brother was a sucker. A good kid. A fucking junior in college. He was going to do great things—join me in the business. But he met her, and he wouldn't listen.

They got married six weeks later without telling anyone. When we found out and tried to talk him into annulling it, he dug in his heels. Joined that damn church and moved out of the city. Five years later, they ended up in Papua fucking New Guinea, and we all know how that ended. She as good as killed him herself. He never would've been there if not for her."

His words twist in a riot in my head, and I'm trying to make sense of them, but it sounds like complete fiction. It can't be true.

"You're telling me that David Karas was not my biological father."

Damon is stone-faced. "No. He wasn't."

My father was not my father. The realization pounds into my brain over and over. I turn and pace toward the door. Several beats later, I gather myself and face him again.

"But he's Greer's father, because she was born in Papua New Guinea."

"Unless your whore mother—"

I bolt across the room and my hand is at his throat, slamming him against the wall. "Shut your fucking mouth."

"Get your hands off me," he forces out through the chokehold.

"Tell me who my father is."

"Let me go."

"I said—" I wrap my fingers tighter around his throat. "Tell me who my fucking father is. You have to know."

Damon's face is turning purple, but he snarls out, "A capo in La Casa Nostra."

I release him, and he stumbles back into the wall.

What the fuck? The *Mafia*?

"You're lying."

"No reason to lie."

I lift my hand to my face as I try to let it sink in. "You have proof?"

He nods. "DNA test. Pulled strings when you were a kid."

The man either has bigger balls than I could have ever suspected—or he's stupid. "How did you not end up dead?"

Damon tries to chuckle, but it comes out as a grunt. He rubs his throat. "I know people."

"Well, you can go fuck yourself. This stays between us. I'm not changing my name. You take that request and shove it up your ass."

"Then get ready to lose your entire company. I will drag you through court and destroy your reputation by dissecting every move you've ever made. I'll be so far up your ass, you'll taste me with every breath."

I have no doubt that he will attempt everything he's saying. The crazy light in his eyes has settled over the expression on his face, and it's clear that logic has fled his mind completely.

"You're going to cost yourself everything. You won't walk away clean from this."

"I don't care," he roars. "I'm going to be a thorn in your side for the rest of your fucking life, like you've been a thorn in mine!"

My hands curl into fists, and I ask the question burning within me. "Why? And if all you want from me is to change my name, why wait until now? Why not earlier?"

Damon's face twists into a sneer. "Every time I miss my brother—his birthday, our annual fishing trip, the World fucking Series, every time I see your goddamn picture in the paper, it makes me sick. If you didn't exist, I'd still have him. It would be a fair trade, in my mind. And since I can't have him back, it gives me some small measure of satisfaction to know that I can make you even a fraction as miserable as I am for losing him."

I squeeze my eyes shut for a beat as a wave of grief hits me. Because the man that my uncle still mourns is one I miss just as much, and had even fewer years with.

"There's something so fucked up about that, I don't even know where to begin. You need help."

He chuckles humorlessly. "No one can bring him back. And now you've proven that blood will always tell. Your mother was trash, and now you've married trash. You've tarnished the family name with your stunt, and I'm done sharing it with you. I won't stop until I win."

His last statement is a vow, and I know that all the words in the world won't change his mind. The man has been buried in the grief of his loss for so many years, it seems to have twisted his mind.

So I don't respond to his dig as I cross the room and rip the door open. My time will be better spent developing a new strategy now that I know what I'm facing. My eyes have reduced to tunnel vision, and I barely notice Elisabetta wringing her hands as I stride for the entrance.

Sliding in the backseat of the Bentley, I tell Michael,

"Let's go home. And hurry."

Because I sure as fuck didn't get the answers I came for.

No, I got my world rocked, and a completely new identity.

CHAPTER
TWENTY-TWO

Holly

Crey enters the penthouse, and it doesn't take a genius to know immediately that something is very, very wrong.

"Crey?"

His hair is wild. His eyes are wild. His entire demeanor is wild. I've never seen him like this, and it sets my stomach on a high-speed churn.

"What happened? Is it bad? He didn't take your deal?"

He walks past me to the window and presses a hand to the glass. His forehead follows next. "My father wasn't my father." His words are so quiet, I can barely make them out.

"What?" I whisper.

"My mother was pregnant when they met."

A lifetime of not knowing who my father is has had a massive impact on me, but just learning it? I can't imagine how much it would throw a person's world off its axis.

"Oh my God. Do you know who . . . ?"

"Not exactly."

I press both hands to my face before rubbing upward and dragging them through my hair.

Holy. Crap.

I cross to his side, wanting nothing more than to offer what little comfort I may be able to. His slumped shoulders look like they're carrying the weight of the world.

"But Damon did tell me he was married, and he was in the Mafia."

"What!" I don't mean to yell, but if ever there was a time to yell, I think this qualifies.

Crey pushes off the glass and turns to me. "Yeah. Apparently I'm half Sicilian and not half Greek."

I study him. "I guess I can see it. But holy shit, Crey. Holy shit. You can't make this shit up. I mean, holy shit."

The edges of his lips curl up in the tiniest hint of a smile, and incredibly, he bursts into a laugh.

"Fuck me, I know. Damon said he was a capo, and that was before I was born. He's probably dead or in prison now. But Jesus fucking Christ. I went to buy back stock in my own company, not a place in the Five Families."

My eyes feel like they may bug out of my head. I'm sure it's not an attractive look on me, but I can't help it. This is so freaking unbelievable.

"This is like real *Godfather*-type shit, isn't it?"

Crey shakes his head. "It changes nothing. I'm still exactly the same man. I'm a product of my experiences. The source of my DNA doesn't change me. And I'm sure as shit not changing my last name."

"Why would you change your last name?" I'm totally confused now.

"That was Damon's price to leave me—to leave us—alone."

"What an arrogant asshole!"

"Calm down, baby," Crey says, reaching for my hand.

I shake him off. "Fuck calming down. I'm about to go backwoods on his ass. I like my new last name. I may not be using it onstage, but I'm sure as hell not giving it up now."

Now Crey's smile threatens to split his face wide. "You are an amazing woman. If anyone had told me that I'd be smiling this soon after having the foundation of my entire existence rocked, I would've told them they were insane. Because I remember, with startling clarity, you telling me that I was under no circumstances to call you *Mrs. Creighton Karas* again, or I'd be at risk of being immortalized in a song about a nutless wonder."

"You do listen." I'm grinning now. "And that was purely a matter of your *this is my woman, and I own her like property* tone at the time that I took exception to. It had nothing to do with your name."

Crey grabs me and hauls me against his chest. I swear I can feel the tension leave his body as soon as it connects with mine.

"This is what I needed. You. In my arms. God, now I'm really tempted to consider Cannon's suggestion about

172

taking a hit out on Damon."

I crane my neck back and look up at him. "That's the Mafioso blood in you talking now, baby. I like it."

"Well, right now I just want to forget this entire morning."

His lips descend on mine, and our mouths meet and devour each other. My tongue finds his and tangles, tastes, and teases. I wrap my arms around his neck and pull myself off my feet before twining my legs about his waist. Crey cradles my ass in both hands and heads for the bedroom.

We're two steps from the door before a knock interrupts us.

I pull back, but Crey says, "Ignore it."

"We can't ignore it. You know it's Cannon, and if he left the Investor Day festivities, it's got to be important."

"You're more important."

I wiggle out of his hold and shimmy down his body, stopping to look down at the tent he's sporting in his suit pants. "How about I get the door?"

Crey shoves a hand through his hair. "Fine," he says, scowling. "But tell him he's an asshole for interrupting."

"I will."

He's shaking his head as I turn away and head to the door. I'm still laughing when I pull it open.

I stop laughing, because it's not Cannon. I have to stop and smooth my hair because I think I'm about to meet my new sister-in-law.

CHAPTER
TWENTY-THREE

Creighton

"Crey! What the hell is going on?" My sister bursts into the penthouse, leaving Holly standing with her hand on the door.

"Greer, meet Holly. Holly, Greer."

Greer spins, holding out a hand. "I'm so sorry. I'm not usually so rude. But normally my aunt doesn't call me to tell me you're my half brother and your dad is a mobster."

Holly takes Greer's hand and shakes it. "Don't worry, we're still absorbing the news."

My sister rushes toward me, her suit jacket buttoned wrong and her eyes wild. "Seriously? What the hell is going on?"

"It's okay, Gree. You probably know just as much as we do at this point." I'm surprised my aunt called her, though.

"You said Aunt Katherine told you? That's shocking."

Greer shakes her head. "She was damn near incoherent, and I'm assuming near the bottom of a bottle of something. She rambled about never approving of how he treated you, and that you had no control over what your mother did. Sins of the father; blah, blah, blah. I just needed to make sure you weren't freaking out and getting ready to kill Uncle Damon or something."

"I'm still working out a solution," I say, but the power flashes twice and the entire penthouse goes dark. The overcast sky barely illuminates beyond the windows.

"Well, shit. Now I'm going to have to take the stairs when I leave. Do you have to live on the top floor, Crey?"

"It'll come back on in a second. The building has a backup generator." As Holly comes toward me and tucks herself against my side, my tone is wry as I say, "I'm sorry you two had to meet like this. I'd anticipated something a little less . . . dramatic."

Holly's soft laugh reaches my ears and calms me further. Even in the midst of craziness, she's a calm place to land, it seems. "I have a feeling our lives are going to be dramatic for a while."

"Not mine," Greer says. "Mine is boring and is going to stay boring. No freaking missed connections gone viral for this girl."

I raise an eyebrow, although in the dark, Greer can't see it. Her words make me hope that the boyfriend who I absolutely don't think is good enough for her won't last long. If I do have those Mafia ties, maybe we could—

The power flashes back on, and Holly and Greer

scream.

"That's it," Holly says. "I'm done with New York. People walk through walls here? Hell. No."

I stiffen and pull Holly closer as my gaze lands on three men standing inside the doorway. They're all imposing, but the one in the center draws my eye.

The likeness is eerie, but not identical, and yet I feel as if I'm staring into the eyes of a much older version of me. About thirty years older, if I have to guess. He has gray eyes, where mine are dark, and I have my mother's fairer skin, instead of his deep olive tone. But the facial features are all there. He's flanked by two men in suits. Bodyguards.

His inspection of me is just as close.

"Creighton." His voice is deep and gravelly, also very much like mine, but with a hint of an accent.

"You sure know how to make one hell of an entrance," I say. "I believe I'm at a disadvantage. I know who you are, but not what your name is."

The man steps forward, and the suits move with him.

"Domenico Casso. Dom. And yes, I'm your father."

Just like they did in Damon's study, all my unconscious reactions become conscious. Every pint of blood pumping through my veins. Every cubic inch of oxygen flowing through my lungs. Every contraction of every muscle.

He holds out his hand and I shake it, noting the surreal quality of it all.

I'm shaking my father's hand.

"How did you—?" I don't even finish the question.

Apparently he knows not only where I live, but how to cut the power, get up to a penthouse apartment without permission, and that I just learned of his existence. And that's really fucking creepy. If I learn he can read the thoughts going through my brain at this moment, I'm not sure I'll be all that surprised.

"Elisabetta."

"What?"

"She's kept tabs on you for years. The whole of your life that you've lived with your aunt and uncle. She's one of my people."

The glimpse I got of her wringing her hands filters back through my brain, along with her quiet kindness to me during my childhood. "Elisabetta is on your payroll?"

He nods. "May we come in?"

I have a feeling there's not much of a real question there. They may have helped themselves to entering, but it's interesting that he's maintaining a pretense of manners. This man makes his own rules.

Maybe the apple doesn't fall so far from the tree, after all.

I step back. "Please do."

They file in, and I lead the way to the seating area. When the two men remain standing behind the couch he chooses to sit on, my question comes of its own accord.

"Damon said you were a capo."

Another nod from Domenico. *Dom. My father.*

"That was a long time ago. I've . . . moved up in the family. CEO, if you will."

"Not surprising," Holly whispers, settling beside me on the couch opposite from him.

Dom's gaze lands on her, and he smiles before shifting back to me. "I was happy to hear you found yourself a good woman. Although perhaps a little surprised by how you went about it."

My eyes narrow. "Have you really been keeping tabs on me my whole life?"

He purses his lips and seems to be choosing his words carefully. "Not the first ten years. You were beyond even me then, and you had your parents. But after they passed away and you came back to New York? Yes. I've made sure to keep tabs."

"But why?"

"Because whether you knew it or not, you're my son."

The million-dollar question burns within me, and I have to ask. "Would you ever have told me?"

He lifts his chin and takes a breath, studying me. It's obviously not the first time he's seen me, but I wonder if he's ever seen me this close in person. We could have passed each other on the street dozens of times, and I would have never realized. Trying to comprehend this is like trying to learn string theory on a napkin in a bar after drinking a dozen pints of Guinness.

He shakes his head decisively. "No. I never would've told you. But now that Damon has run his mouth, I had no choice but to intervene."

"An inconvenience, I'm sure," I say, my tone dry.

"One I was ready for. I'm actually surprised he's held it in this long. Elisabetta has been waiting twenty-some years to make this call. But the timing works in your favor, as well as mine."

"What do you mean?" If he's talking in Mafia code

speak, I'm not following.

"He used his connections a long time ago to get information he should never have had. I knew he had it, and as long as he did nothing with it, I would do nothing with him. But he's broken the balance, and it must be righted."

Holly stiffens against my side, her hand landing on my knee and squeezing. "I'm sorry, Dom. We're going to need to rewind the last thirty seconds and pretend we didn't hear that."

I cover Holly's hand with mine. "I think you should go in the other room."

Her nails dig into my leg. "Not a chance."

One of the bodyguards snorts, but silences it immediately.

"Holly—"

"Crey—"

"Children, children," Dom says. "The last thing I want is to cause marital strife. After having thirty years with my own wife, I can understand that these early days are delicate."

Holly shoots a glance at him, and I know exactly what she's thinking.

"Holly."

"Crey."

Dom smiles. "Yes. I know what she's thinking, as well. And no, I wasn't faithful to my wife. I should regret that, but then your husband wouldn't exist. So, Mrs. Karas, how would you like me to respond?"

Holly must be gritting her teeth, because she says nothing.

Dom turns his focus to me and continues. "I understand your hesitance to know anything about my plans for Damon. That's fine. But my world is not your world. A move like his cannot go unchecked. I stay in my position by exercising iron-clad control over my domain."

I shake my head. "I want his shares back; I don't want him dead. The problem with him ending up dead is that I'll be the prime suspect, regardless of how it happens. We're in the middle of one shitstorm right now, but it's a corporate litigation matter. A criminal investigation and potential charges would be a whole different ball game, and I want nothing to do with that. If my stock price has taken a hit from the derivative suit, it's nothing compared to what would happen if I were questioned in Damon's disappearance or murder."

Dom leans back and spreads his arms over the back of the couch, looking every inch the Mafia boss. All he needs is a stogie and a cloud of smoke to complete the picture.

"You raise a good point." He brings a hand to his chin and scratches it as flashes of classic mob movies run through my head. "Hmm, you say you just want your shares back? That solves your problem?"

"Yes. The lawsuit goes away if he's not a shareholder to maintain it," I explain.

"After the suit has been dropped a while, I'm assuming you don't care what happens to him?" he asks.

"I didn't say that. He wasn't a complete dick to Greer, and it would hurt her to lose him." I glance at my sister, who has stayed oddly silent on the far side of the room. Her eyes are wide.

Dom looks her way as well. "I assumed that's who has been watching me so closely. It's lovely to meet you, Greer."

Greer uncrosses her arms and nods. "Likewise, I'm sure." She shocks me by adding, "I've seen you before. With the two guard dogs. In Midtown one night when I was leaving work."

Dom lifts his chin. "You take too many chances with your safety, Ms. Karas. You've been lucky my men have been keeping tabs and have intervened on your behalf."

Holly stiffens beside me, and the color drains from Greer's face.

"What?"

"I extend my protection to you out of courtesy to your brother because I know it would trouble him for you to be injured. But that's no reason to be so careless."

My insides, which have already taken a beating today, once again turn cold.

"Fuck." I lift my hand from Holly's and scrub it over my face. "Greer, you're getting a bodyguard. Don't argue with me. It's happening."

Greer opens her mouth to protest, but I glare her into silence. Her lips snap shut.

"I'm happy to recommend some competent ones," Dom says, a condescending smile on his face.

"I'll take care of it, but thank you for the offer."

Once again, he gives me what I now think of as the *Dom nod*. "Now about Damon. You'll have his stock certificate in hand tomorrow. Consider it a belated wedding present."

He stands and glances at Holly. "I'll be keeping tabs

on your mother, as well. If she gets out of line again, we'll make sure she's encouraged to not make the same mistake again. I believe that concludes our business."

Holly speaks up. "You're not going to . . ."

He laughs. "No. But she won't be a problem." Dom nods at both of us, and then looks to Greer. "It was nice to finally meet you. I don't expect we'll see each other again." His gaze lands on me again. "And if you're wondering, the wiring in your building has malfunctioned mysteriously, and we were never here."

Holly sucks in an audible breath, and I raise a brow. "And the doorman and other residents?"

He cocks his head. "We didn't exactly use the front door. We'll see ourselves out. Take care, Creighton. It was lovely to meet you, Holly. Good luck at the CMAs."

We stand in stunned silence while the room once again goes dark, and the mob boss—my father—exits our life with his two bodyguards just as quickly as he entered it.

As soon as the door shuts behind them, Holly loses it. "Holy cow, Creighton. Holy cow-tipping, runnin' from the cops, falling into a pile of shit. Oh my God, did that really just happen?"

From Greer, I hear a hushed, "Holy fucking shit."

"Do you think you'll ever see him again?" Holly asks.

The lights come back on, and I blink a few times before replying. "I have no idea. But my guess is, not unless he wants me to."

I'm still trying to comprehend everything that I've learned in the last couple of hours. It's surreal. The man I thought was my biological father was not. All the hatred that has come from my uncle all these years has nothing to do with me, and everything to do with his own fucked-up issues. So, one burden lifted and another burden dropped like a wrecking ball through the very fabric of my existence.

Greer crosses toward us. "As much as I'm a little freaked out right now to leave your place, I gotta go."

I hug my sister, and as she steps away, I tell her, "You're getting a bodyguard. No more walking around Manhattan late at night because you don't leave work until two a.m."

"I'm not going to win this one, am I?" she asks.

"No."

"I respectfully reserve the right to argue the point later."

"Spoken like a lawyer. I'm calling Michael. He'll be waiting downstairs in less than ten minutes. Don't leave the building until you see him pull up."

Greer sucks in a long breath. "Fine." She raises on tiptoe to press a kiss to my cheek. "Call me if anything crazy happens."

I ruffle her hair. "Of course. Now, go."

Once my sister closes the door behind her, Holly and I are left standing in the middle of the penthouse, staring at each other. She breaks the silence first.

"Are we still on for Vegas?"

Not where I thought she'd start the conversation, but a good choice nonetheless. I've never wanted to get out of New York so badly in my life.

"Hell yes."

She smiles. "Good. Then I have one more question."

Her smile loosens something within me, and I feel my own lips curl up at the edges.

"What, baby?"

"Does that make you a Mafia prince? I'm not trying to make light of the situation." She holds up a hand. "I swear, I'm not. Because this is crazy and emotional and intense. And just plain crazy. But that Mafia prince thing . . . if you're down for some role-play when we're in Vegas, I'm not going to say no to that."

My chest shakes with bubbling laughter, and the most insane situation I've ever faced in my entire life dissolves away for the moment because of the quirky, amazing, gorgeous woman in front of me.

I drop a hand on each of her shoulders. "Let's see what happens when we get to Vegas."

CHAPTER
TWENTY-FOUR

Holly

"Karas International stock has risen sharply following the news that the shareholder suit against its chief executive officer, Creighton Karas, was dropped earlier this week. Karas commented from the floor of Caesar's Palace, where he stood at his wife's side during her run on the craps table. 'I'm happy to see that my uncle understands that the health of the company is more important than any grudge he has against me personally. We're looking forward to another record-breaking year in profits.' There's no doubt the world will be watching Karas International, and its CEO, closely in the coming months."

I reach for the radio and flip it from the news station to my favorite channel, *The Highway*, which features up-

and-coming country artists mixed in with all the old favorites.

"Glad they got the part about the craps table in there," Creighton says.

"And that Dom was as good as his word," I add.

Creighton lays an arm across the back of my seat. "Yes, yes he was. Now let's get the hell out of here."

I smile and shift my new Mustang into gear. After Creighton showed me the basics of craps and dared me to lose ten grand, I threw myself into the game wholeheartedly. But I wasn't able to lose. Nope, I just kept winning, at least until my inner Kentucky girl realized that I could buy a damn car with what I won, and I politely cashed out and walked away with my money.

When we landed in Nashville, I told Creighton I wanted to buy a new car. He asked the driver to take us to the Maserati dealer, but I vetoed his choice in favor of stopping at the Ford dealership. My one concession was allowing him to drag me out of the used-car section to look at the new ones—and I fell in love with a Shelby GT350. It was delivered this morning to the penthouse condo we're temporarily staying in until we can find a house we both love.

So, the first order of business today is stopping at the studio to finish recording the last of my new songs, and then house hunting.

I floor the Mustang, my laughter echoing in the cabin as Creighton grabs the oh-shit handle above his seat. I'm pretty sure the man is not going to let me drive much, because he doesn't seem to approve of my newly adopted *drive it like you stole it* style.

When we arrive at the studio—in record time and all in one piece, I might add—Creighton lays a hand over mine on the gearshift.

"Are you sure you don't want a driver?"

I tilt my head. "You're going to lose on this one. I promise."

He narrows his eyes, and a low sound that mimics a growl comes from his side of the car. "Holly . . ."

"It'll be fine. I swear. I'm just seeing what she can do."

"She?"

With my free hand, I pet the steering wheel. "Of course it's a she. Her name is Cherry Bomb."

Creighton shakes his head with an indulgent smile. "If you name my cock . . ."

I raise an eyebrow. "Who says I haven't?"

His gaze sharpens on mine. "You're not going to tell me, are you?"

My smile threatens to split my face. "Nope," I reply, making sure to pop the *p*. "You'll just have to wonder."

"Oh, you'll tell me. I have my ways."

I let another laugh break free as I push open my door.

I meet my band in the studio, hugging each of the guys while Creighton shakes their hands. We haven't seen them since the tour wrapped up, and I think they're as anxious to lay these tracks down as I am. Once inside the recording booth, I sling Eliza Belle's strap over my shoulder, and we spend the next several hours getting everything but the vocals recorded.

After a break for lunch, it's time to finish up. My gaze darts to the glass window of the booth where Creighton leans against the wall just beyond. He's never heard the lyrics to this one, and I wonder how he's going to react.

The tracks we just laid down play through my headphones and I start to sing. Normally I tend to record with my eyes shut, feeling every note with my entire body, but today, I can't help but stare into the eyes of the man I love.

When we get to the end of the chorus, I let loose with everything I have in me.

> *I thought I'd be lost on Fifth Avenue,*
> *but I was only lost until I found you.*

When we finish recording, I remove my headphones and make my way out of the booth. Creighton hasn't moved from where he's leaning against the wall. As I walk closer, I note the glassy sheen in his eyes.

When he speaks, his words are low so only I can hear them.

"I was the one who was lost. I just didn't know it until I found you." He reaches for my hand and pulls me close. "I love you so goddamn much, Holly. I never want to go back to being that man."

I reach up with my free hand and wrap it around his neck. It's amazing to see how much my husband has changed since Christmas Eve. Yes, he'll always be demanding, dominant, and deliciously dirty, but the intensity of the feelings underpinning all of those things makes all the difference in the world.

"I'll never let you go back to being that man, because I'm never giving you up, Creighton Karas. I love you. You're mine. Always."

I lean up to press my lips to his, and he threads his fingers into my hair, deepening the kiss. When I finally pull back, I meet his gaze as it burns into mine.

"Mine. Always," he says. "Now, let's go find our new home."

Home. When he says the word, I realize that mine is wherever Creighton is. It could be Nashville, New York, or New Delhi, but as long as he's there, I'm home.

EPILOGUE

Creighton

Nine months later

Watching Holly climb to the stage in her glittering gold dress to accept the New Artist of the Year award from my seat in the arena is surreal. I've made a habit of winning in my life. Winning the game. Winning the bet. Winning the deal. Winning the woman. But nothing compares to watching her win this award.

Nothing.

I've found contentment in my life, despite the whirlwind it now resembles as I try to keep up with both my schedule and Holly's. Although honestly, I've backed off a lot from mine and handed off as much as possible to Cannon. He's kicking ass and taking names, and has groomed a sidekick of his own.

These days, Holly and I are spending more and more

time in Nashville, and less in Manhattan. Our place in Tennessee is feeling more like home than the penthouse in the city, mostly because Holly loves it so much. She has also stretched her wings in the business world as well. She's not CEO of Homegrown Records, but she's been involved in a lot of the business decisions. Her practical nature and straight-up cheapskate attitude is exactly what that place needs to get back in the black.

I spin the titanium ring on my left hand, following Holly's every movement as she accepts the polished crystal award and congratulatory hugs from the presenters.

She gave me the ring a few days after I first heard the lyrics to "Lost on Fifth Avenue," the song that rocked the charts—and netted her the award she's about to accept. On the inside of the band, the words *Lost until I found you* were engraved. She said it wasn't about telling the world I was taken, but about carrying a piece of her with me everywhere I went. Someone will have to pry that ring off my cold, dead body, because I'll never take it off otherwise.

Holly steps up to the microphone with a brilliant smile, her left hand hovering over the baby bump the tabloids have been talking about nonstop. This morning, we learned that she's carrying our daughter. There was no argument over her name either. Rosemary Elizabeth Karas, for Holly's grandmother and my mother.

Holly's mother hasn't been seen or heard from since the day she showed up at the gate of our house in Nashville to beg for money after she spent every dime from the *Yammer* payout. Her pleas were met with Holly's "No fucking way on God's green Earth will you get another cent from us," and a threat to call the cops.

Holly waits for the crowd to quiet before she begins her acceptance speech. "Hey, y'all. Thank you so much for this. I can't even tell you how it feels for a girl from Gold Haven, Kentucky, who used to watch this show on the tiny TV in a singlewide trailer, to be standing on this stage accepting it. Surreal doesn't even begin to cover it. I want to thank my husband, Creighton Karas, a man insane enough to place a missed connection ad looking for a one-night stand."

The entire audience bursts into laughter at Holly's blunt words.

"Because his insanity is the best damn thing that's ever happened to me. I would've never written the songs on the album without it, and the single that got me your votes would've never come to be if I hadn't met him. I love you, Crey. This is for you. It's all for you."

She holds the award over her head for a moment before lowering it and continuing. "I'd also like to thank my agent, my manager, and my very own label, Homegrown Records. This past year has been absolutely amazing. Thank you all."

She steps toward backstage, and I rise to slip down the aisle and around back of the arena to meet her. Holly doesn't know it, but following the after party, the jet is waiting on the tarmac to take us on our actual honeymoon. It may have been delayed a while due to our busy schedules, but three weeks in Bora Bora without Internet is exactly what we need. I've got new journals for her and her guitar already packed. Along with a few bikinis.

She's posing for pictures when I get backstage, the award gripped in her hand.

Holly turns her head mid-pose while the dozen or so cameras continue flashing. She doesn't even care that she's screwing up all of their shots, because she's caught sight of me.

"Excuse me. Can you give me a minute? Oh, and hold this." She shoves the award into the hands of some random photographer. He drops his camera, which is luckily caught by the strap around his neck, and clutches the award to his chest.

Holly doesn't even wait to see if he's going to drop the thing; she just runs toward me. And when I say *runs toward me,* I mean she launches herself off the heels of her tall boots toward me. I catch her, wrapping my hands around her waist and holding her up, because she can't twine her legs around me like she normally would, given the dress she's wearing.

"I did it! I really, really did it!"

"Yeah, you did, baby. You sure did. Congratulations, Holly. You earned it."

Her arms wrap around my neck, and she whispers, "I think you need to get me out of here because I'm about to ugly cry."

My heart clenches at the rich tide of emotion underpinning her words. "Baby, it's okay."

Holly lifts her head, and sure enough, tears are already gathering in her eyes. "You need to get that award, and we need to get the hell out of Dodge."

"You really want me to make our excuses?"

She nods vigorously. "Okay."

I take two steps to the photographer, who is already holding out the award. "Thank you. Is there an empty room around here?"

His eyes bulge dangerously close to out of his head. "Uh . . . uh . . . That way." He points to the right with the award. "Around the corner and down the hall. Try the second door on the left."

"Thank you," I say, swinging Holly up in my arms like a bride. Her face is still tucked into my neck. "Reach out a hand and grab the award, baby," I say under my breath.

Holly complies, and I head in the direction the photographer indicated. When I find the room, I shoulder open the door and fumble for the light switch. It turns out to be a dressing room, much like so many others I've been in with Holly. I lower us onto a couch, and try not to think about the number of groupies who've been fucked on it. Taking the award from Holly's hand, I set it safely aside.

That's when the tears start falling. Happy tears, I hope.

Holly shakes against me, and I hold her tighter.

"I can't believe it's real. It just doesn't seem like it could be real." She swallows back a sob, and I rub her back.

"It's real. And you earned it. You worked your ass off to get here. It's as real as it gets." At my last words, she lifts her tearstained face.

"As real as it gets? That's what you said about us before."

"Yeah, I guess I did."

"Took me a while to believe that too."

"I have a feeling you'll believe this one sooner. After

194

all, you've got the trophy to prove it."

She shakes her head. "The real prize here is you."

When I lean down to press my lips to hers, I whisper, "We're the prize. The absolute best fucking prize of my life." I stand and swing her into my arms again. "Now, what do you say about a honeymoon before this baby starts running our lives?"

Holly blinks, and a mischievous smile spreads across her face. "A honeymoon? Where are you taking me?"

"Does it matter?"

She moves her head from side to side, shaking it slowly. "I'll go anywhere with you, Mr. Karas. Take me away."

The End

You know you don't want to miss what's coming next! Click here (http://www.meghanmarch.com/#!newsletter/c1uhp) to sign up for my newsletter, and never miss another announcement about upcoming projects, new releases, sales, exclusive excerpts, and giveaways.

I'd love to hear what you thought about Holly and Creighton's story. If you have a few moments to leave a review, I'd be incredibly grateful. Send me a link at meghanmarchbooks@gmail.com, and I'll thank you with a personal note.

Also by Meghan March

THE DIRTY BILLIONAIRE Trilogy:
Dirty Billionaire
Dirty Pleasures
Dirty Together

BENEATH Series:
Beneath This Mask
Beneath This Ink
Beneath These Chains
Beneath These Scars

FLASH BANG Series:
Flash Bang
Hard Charger

Author's Note

I'd love to hear from you. Connect with me at:

UNAPOLOGETICALLY SEXY ROMANCE

Website: www.meghanmarch.com

Facebook: www.facebook.com/MeghanMarchAuthor

Twitter: www.twitter.com/meghan_march

Instagram: www.instagram.com/meghanmarch

ABOUT THE AUTHOR

Meghan March has been known to wear camo face paint and tromp around in the woods wearing mud-covered boots, all while sporting a perfect manicure. She's also impulsive, easily entertained, and absolutely unapologetic about the fact that she loves to read and write smut.

Her past lives include slinging auto parts, selling lingerie, making custom jewelry, and practicing corporate law. Writing books about dirty-talking alpha males and the strong, sassy women who bring them to their knees is by far the most fabulous job she's ever had.

She loves hearing from her readers at:
meghanmarchbooks@gmail.com